Enjoy all of these American Girl Mysteries®:

THE SILENT STRANGER   A *Kaya* Mystery

LADY MARGARET'S GHOST   A *Felicity* Mystery

SECRETS IN THE HILLS   A *Josefina* Mystery

THE CAMEO NECKLACE   A *Cécile* Mystery

THE RUNAWAY FRIEND   A *Kirsten* Mystery

SHADOWS ON SOCIETY HILL   An *Addy* Mystery

CLUES IN THE CASTLE TOWER   A *Samantha* Mystery

THE CRYSTAL BALL   A *Rebecca* Mystery

MISSING GRACE   A *Kit* Mystery

CLUES IN THE SHADOWS   A *Molly* Mystery

THE SILVER GUITAR   A *Julie* Mystery

and many more!

— A *Marie-Grace* MYSTERY —

THE
HIDDEN GOLD

by Sarah Masters Buckey

★ American Girl®

Questions or comments? Call 1-800-845-0005, visit **americangirl.com**,
or write to Customer Service, American Girl, 8400 Fairway Place,
Middleton, WI 53562-0497.

Printed in China
12 13 14 15 16 17 LEO 10 9 8 7 6 5 4 3 2 1

PICTURE CREDITS
The following individuals and organizations have generously
given permission to reprint illustrations contained in "Looking Back":
pp. 142–143—English School/The Bridgeman Art Library/Getty Images
(steamboat); courtesy of the Historic New Orleans Collection (interior of a
steamboat); pp. 144–145—courtesy of the Historic New Orleans Collection
(port of New Orleans); *Loading Cotton on the Mississippi*, 1870, by Currier & Ives
(steamboat); Marie Adrien Persac (Franco-American, 1823–73) *Interior of the
Steamship Princess/Imperial*, 1861, gouache and collage on paper, 17 x 22 15/16
inches. LSU Museum of Art 75.8. gift of Mrs. Mamie Persac Lusk. Photography:
David Humphreys (steamboat saloon); pp. 146–147—Courtesy of Mr. L. J. Persac
Jr. (vase); courtesy of Cornell University Library, Making of America Digital
Collection (men playing cards); *Wooding Up on the Mississippi*, 1863 (Day Version)
by Francis F. Palmer (steamboat getting wood); MHP Enterprises, Inc., Salem, MA
(steamboat and raft at night); pp. 148–149—North Wind Picture Archives
(view from pilothouse); Library of Congress, LC-USZ62-5513 (Mark Twain).

Illustrations by Sergio Giovine

Cataloging-in-Publication data
available from the Library of Congress

For my niece, Nicole

In 1854, many people and places in New Orleans had French names. You'll see some French names in this book. Look in the glossary on page 150 for help in pronouncing the names.

TABLE OF CONTENTS

1 AN UNEXPECTED TRAVELER 1

2 GOLD RUSH 16

3 A WARNING 32

4 RIDDLES AND RHYMES 47

5 CLUES IN THE PAGES 53

6 PANIC AT NIGHT 63

7 MISSING 74

8 HITTING A SNAG 84

9 A GAMBLE 96

10 LOST AND FOUND 108

11 MAGIC NIGHT 114

12 DESPERATE SEARCH 123

13 THE KEY 130

    LOOKING BACK 142

    GLOSSARY OF FRENCH NAMES 150

1

AN UNEXPECTED TRAVELER

In her tiny stateroom aboard the steamboat *Liberty*, Marie-Grace Gardner carefully set her inkwell on the table beside her bed. Then she dipped her pen in the ink and wrote,

Monday, March 13, 1854

Dear Cécile,
My papa and I came aboard this morning. The crew is still loading cargo on the boat, but Papa says we'll be leaving New Orleans soon. The Liberty *is the biggest steamboat I've ever seen. The main cabin is as fancy as the ballrooms at the Grand Théâtre.*

As she dipped her pen again, Marie-Grace smiled to herself. She was sure that Cécile would remember the elegant building where they'd had their first adventure together.

*There's a little girl named Annabelle Rumsford
on board. Her mama asked if I'd play with her this
morning. While Annabelle and I were on deck, I saw
an artist painting pictures of the river. It reminded me
of your brother Armand. I hope*

Marie-Grace stopped in mid-sentence as the
door to her stateroom swung open.

"I found you, Marie-Grace!" a little girl with
blonde curls declared triumphantly. Holding her
rag doll, Priscilla, close by her side, Annabelle
rushed into the room and plopped herself down
on the bed, right next to Marie-Grace.

Oh dear, thought Marie-Grace. Annabelle was
a cheerful little girl, full of energy and eager to
play. Marie-Grace was happy to spend time with
her, but right now she wanted to finish her letter.

"Hello, Annabelle," Marie-Grace greeted her.
"Are you finished with your nap already?"

"I wasn't tired at all, so Mama said I could get
up." She leaned over the letter that Marie-Grace

was writing, and her elbow smudged the fresh ink. "What are you doing?"

"Writing a letter," Marie-Grace said, moving the paper out of Annabelle's reach.

"I want to write a letter, too!" said Annabelle, swinging her legs from the edge of the bed. "May I use your pen? Please?"

Marie-Grace hesitated. Her stateroom wasn't much bigger than a large closet, but it was freshly painted and very pretty. There were two narrow beds set into the wall, one on top of the other. Both berths had white embroidered covers, and there was a delicate white cloth on the bedside table. Marie-Grace had already noticed that Annabelle was apt to get into mischief. So far this morning, the little girl had accidentally knocked over a bucket of water on the deck, and then, when she was running to tell her mother, she had slipped and fallen in the puddle she had made.

If Annabelle spills ink in here, I'll never be able to clean it up, thought Marie-Grace. "I'll finish my letter later," she told Annabelle. Marie-Grace put the cork back into the ink bottle and tucked it

3

inside her trunk, along with the letter.

For a moment, Annabelle's blue eyes clouded with disappointment. Then she brightened. "Let's go out on the deck again and throw bread."

Marie-Grace and Annabelle had fed the gulls earlier, and Marie-Grace still had one thick crust of bread left. "All right," she agreed as the steamboat's bell clanged. "We'll be sailing soon, and then there won't be as many birds."

Annabelle grinned and hurried to the open door. "Mama!" she called. "Marie-Grace said she'll take me to feed the birds again."

"I'll be there in a moment, too, dear," Mrs. Rumsford answered from the room next door.

Marie-Grace could hear Annabelle's baby sister crying. She guessed that Mrs. Rumsford was glad to have help with Annabelle. "Let's go," said Marie-Grace, holding out her hand to the little girl.

Each stateroom on the *Liberty* had two doors. One led into the main cabin of the steamboat. The other door opened onto one of the galleries that ran along the outside of the boat like long balconies, overlooking the river. Marie-Grace opened the door to the gallery, and the girls stepped outside.

The *Liberty* was one of many boats docked along the busy, noisy New Orleans levee. Other steamboats were already sailing on the river, along with rafts, small fishing boats, and some old-fashioned flatboats loaded with cargo. *Soon we'll be on our way, too,* thought Marie-Grace with a thrill of anticipation.

She'd been on the Mississippi River before, when she had traveled with Uncle Luc and Aunt Océane to visit family. That had been a wonderful trip, but they had sailed only a short way. On this trip, Marie-Grace and her father were going to travel all the way from New Orleans to Cairo, Illinois. From Cairo, they would take another steamboat up the Ohio River to Pennsylvania, where they would visit old friends of Papa's before returning to New Orleans.

When Marie-Grace had told Cécile about the trip, her friend had made her promise to write as often as she could. "Tell me all about your adventures!" she'd urged Marie-Grace.

Marie-Grace had hesitated. "What if nothing exciting happens?"

"Oh, something will!" Cécile had insisted with her usual confidence. "Just don't forget to write me about it."

Now as she and Annabelle walked toward the open promenade area at the front of the steamboat, Marie-Grace decided that she would tell her friend all about the *Liberty*. *I bet Cécile's never been on a boat this big either,* she thought.

The steam engines on the *Liberty* powered two huge paddle wheels, one on the *starboard* or right side of the boat, the other on the *port* or left side. The magnificent boat was painted white with blue trim. It had three full decks and a pair of tall smokestacks that rose high into the sky.

When she and Papa had arrived on the *Liberty*, Marie-Grace had seen that each of the steamboat's decks was very different. The first or main deck was crowded with cargo. Lots of people were on this deck, too. Some were crew members who were busy hauling crates and sacks and barrels on board. Others were passengers who traveled on the main deck, even though there were no staterooms or sleeping berths on this level. The main-deck passengers were able to get cheap tickets because they slept amid the cargo or on the open deck during the entire trip.

The middle deck was called the boiler deck, and it was much fancier. Passengers paid more for their tickets, but they had private staterooms with comfortable beds. There were carved guardrails along the outside of the boiler deck, and passengers could sit or stroll along the galleries. Stateroom passengers, like Marie-Grace and her father, also enjoyed meals in the steamboat's elegant main cabin.

The boat's captain, two pilots, and other officers had their living quarters on the hurricane deck, which was above the boiler deck. Perched at the top of the *Liberty* was the pilothouse, where the steamboat's pilots steered the huge boat.

This afternoon, Captain Obadiah Smith was standing with a dozen or so passengers on the boiler deck, watching the cargo being loaded on the main deck below. Mr. Stevenson, one of the pilots, was on the deck, too, along with Marie-Grace's father, Dr. Thaddeus Gardner. Mr. Stevenson was a friend of Papa's. Last summer, Dr. Gardner had taken care of Mr. Stevenson's son when the boy had become sick with yellow fever, the terrible disease that had killed so many people in New Orleans.

Papa had worked long hours during the yellow fever epidemic, and he had often treated patients at Charity Hospital. Two nuns who were traveling on the *Liberty* had worked at the hospital, too, and they greeted Papa as an old friend. Sister Catherine was a tiny, talkative woman, and Sister Frederica was tall and quiet.

While the grown-ups chatted, Marie-Grace and Annabelle took up positions at the front deck rail. Marie-Grace handed Annabelle several small chunks of bread. "When I say 'three,' throw the bread as far as you can!" Marie-Grace reminded her. "One, two, THREE!"

Both girls tossed their bread to the birds.

Squawking, the birds eagerly dived for the chunks. Annabelle giggled. "Let's do that again!"

Mrs. Rumsford, with her baby in her arms, came out on deck as the gulls snapped up the last crumbs of bread. Mrs. Rumsford gave Marie-Grace a smile of thanks. Then she called, "Come, Annabelle. We'll walk the baby out here for a bit."

As Annabelle ran to join her mother, Marie-Grace looked out over the railing toward New Orleans. She could see the spires of St. Louis Cathedral, and even though she was excited about the trip, she felt a pang of sadness at leaving the city. She knew that in the weeks she would be away, she would miss her home, her dog Argos, and all her friends, especially Cécile.

An early spring breeze was blowing as Marie-Grace watched the crowds of people on the shore. Men in dark suits and ladies in bright dresses were hurrying along the levee, rushing to catch boats. Street vendors were crying out the goods they had for sale, and carriage drivers were calling to their horses. Laborers were shouting as they carried cargo to and from the boats. Newly arrived immigrants were clustered along the levee too, many talking in foreign languages.

Above all the noise came the sound of an old man's voice. He was standing by the *Liberty*'s gangplank, arguing with two crew members. A girl in a brown dress stood near the man, and behind her, porters carried two large trunks. *I wonder what's happening?* Marie-Grace thought as the steamboat's bell clanged again.

The elderly man called up to the captain in French-accented English. "May I have a word with you, sir?"

Captain Smith, a tall man with steel-gray hair and thick gray eyebrows, was smoking a pipe. He nodded to the two men at the gangplank, and the crew members stepped aside to allow the new arrivals aboard.

As Marie-Grace and the other passengers looked on curiously, the elderly man came puffing up the stairs from the main deck, followed by the girl and the porters. The man had white hair and a kind face. He introduced himself to Captain Smith as Monsieur LaPlante, owner of a small hotel on Canal Street.

Monsieur LaPlante gestured to the girl. "This young lady is Wilhelmina Newman. Her father was staying at my hotel but, very sadly, he died a few days ago. Now she must travel back to her grandmother in New Madrid, Missouri. Your steamboat will stop there, won't it?"

"Yes," Captain Smith said. He tapped his pipe on the railing. "Does she have a ticket for a stateroom?"

Monsieur LaPlante looked concerned. "Well, the child came to New Orleans as a deck passenger." He gestured to the main deck below. "Could she not travel back on your deck? She has very little money, but she must get back to her home as soon as it can be arranged."

"The deck is no place for a child traveling alone," said the captain. "Besides, most of those passengers have just come from Europe and hardly speak English." Captain Smith shook his head. "If the girl does not have family or friends with her, she'll need a ticket for a stateroom."

The Hidden Gold

"Ah, what a shame!" said Monsieur LaPlante, his shoulders slumping in defeat. "She has no one to take her home. I was told that you were a charitable man and might help the child."

Wilhelmina stepped out from behind Monsieur LaPlante. She was very thin, with red hair and pale skin. She looked tired, but she spoke out boldly. "My ma was German, and I speak a bit of German, too. I could manage all right on the deck."

She said her mother was *German,* Marie-Grace realized. *So* both *of her parents have passed away.* Marie-Grace's own mother had died several years ago, and her heart went out to the girl. *What would it be like for Wilhelmina to travel all by herself?* Marie-Grace wondered. Wilhelmina was wearing a faded brown calico dress with only a light shawl. *Surely she'd be cold on deck. If only there was another place for her to sleep . . .*

With a start, Marie-Grace remembered the extra bed in her tiny stateroom. For a moment, she hesitated. She was shy, and this girl didn't seem very friendly. *But how would I feel if I was in her place?* Marie-Grace wondered. She decided to take a chance. "Wilhelmina can stay with me," she offered quietly.

Captain Smith turned to Marie-Grace. "What did you say?"

Suddenly, everyone was looking at Marie-Grace. She felt her face blush bright red, but forced herself to speak louder this time. "Wilhelmina could share my stateroom," she told the captain. "I wouldn't mind at all."

"What a good idea!" exclaimed one of the passengers. She was a plump woman in a cranberry-colored dress, and she looked at Wilhelmina pityingly. "The child would be much better off in a stateroom."

"It would be an act of charity to take her back to her family," added Sister Catherine, and Sister Frederica nodded in agreement.

Wilhelmina scowled at them. "I'm not a child," she said, lifting her chin. "I turned eleven last month. And I don't want charity—just passage home."

She's my age, thought Marie-Grace. *It would*

be nice to have someone besides Annabelle to talk to.

"It wouldn't be charity. I'd *like* company," Marie-Grace said quickly. "There's an extra bed in my stateroom, too."

Captain Smith tapped his pipe again. "We can find a place for your trunks down on the main deck," he told Wilhelmina. "And if Miss Gardner is willing to share her stateroom, you can travel for free."

Wilhelmina's eyes widened. "I need to have *both* my trunks with me."

"Her father left those trunks for her," Monsieur LaPlante explained.

The captain frowned at the pair of trunks. One was old and caked with dirt. The other was smaller and had shiny brass fittings and a bright brass lock. "There isn't room for both those trunks in the stateroom," he said flatly. He pointed to the smaller one. "You can keep that one, and we'll put the other one with the cargo. We're leaving in a few minutes, so decide whether you want to stay here or come with us."

Dr. Gardner looked at Wilhelmina with

concern. "I urge you to accept Captain Smith's offer," he said

"Indeed, it's a generous offer, child. You could travel back in comfort," Monsieur LaPlante said. "And if you don't leave now, we'll have to find someone else to take you back to your family." The old man wiped his brow. "I don't know how long that will take."

"But I *have* to get home now!" Wilhelmina protested. She looked even paler than before, and she seemed unsteady on her feet.

"Are you feeling ill?" Marie-Grace asked, reaching out a hand to her.

"I'm fine," declared Wilhelmina. She brushed Marie-Grace's hand away. "I guess I'll come with you, but . . ." She closed her eyes and rubbed her forehead. "I, um . . ." Wilhelmina's face turned a sickly shade of white. Then she collapsed in a heap onto the deck.

2
GOLD RUSH

Everyone gathered around the fallen girl.
Sister Frederica cradled her in her arms, and
Dr. Gardner checked her pulse. He turned to
Marie-Grace. "Grace, please get my bag. It's in
my stateroom."

"Yes, Papa," said Marie-Grace. Her father
always carried his medical supplies with him in
a small black bag. Marie-Grace ran to her father's
room and grabbed the bag. She was rushing out
the door again when she almost collided with a
well-dressed young man wearing eyeglasses.

"Excuse me!" said Marie-Grace, hurrying on.

"Can I help you?" asked the young man.

"No—but thank you," Marie-Grace replied.

As soon as Marie-Grace returned with the
bag, Papa dug inside it and pulled out a bottle of

smelling salts. He opened the bottle and waved it under Wilhelmina's nose.

Wilhelmina gagged. "That smells awful!"

"Yes, it does," Papa agreed, putting the top back on the bottle. "But I'm glad you're awake now." He put his hand on her forehead. "You don't seem to have a fever," he added. Papa looked closely at Wilhelmina. "When was the last time you ate a full meal?"

Wilhelmina shrugged. "I don't know."

Maybe she fainted from hunger, Marie-Grace realized. Marie-Grace volunteered at Holy Trinity Orphanage in New Orleans. Sometimes hungry children arrived at the orphanage, and they were often thin and tired looking, like Wilhelmina.

"You need to rest and get plenty of food," Papa told the girl. He helped Wilhelmina to her feet. "Luckily, you'll have a chance to do that on this trip."

"Here's some water," said Sister Catherine, handing her a glass. "Would you like something to eat?"

Wilhelmina took a sip of water. Then she

shook her head. "No, I'm all right," she said.

Marie-Grace saw that Wilhelmina's hand was trembling as she held the glass. "I'm going to my room," Marie-Grace told her. "Do you want to come with me?"

Wilhelmina nodded and gave the glass back to Sister Catherine. Marie-Grace led the way along the gallery. Instead of numbers, the stateroom doors were all labeled with the names of states. Marie-Grace stopped at the brass plaque that said "North Carolina."

"See, there's room here for both of us," Marie-Grace said as she opened the door. She gestured to the two berths. "You can lie down in either bed."

Wilhelmina took off her shawl and settled herself on the bottom berth. "I'm not tired, but I'll sit here for a moment," she said, as if she were doing Marie-Grace a favor. "Then I'll go see about my trunks."

"All right," Marie-Grace said. She had hoped that she and Wilhelmina could become friends, but Wilhelmina didn't seem friendly at all. *She's only just lost her father*, Marie-Grace told herself. *Maybe she wants to be alone.*

The silence was awkward in the small room. Marie-Grace decided to keep busy by unpacking her trunk. She unfolded two shawls and a pair of petticoats, and then she took out her most prized possession, her silver-framed portrait of her mother. As she placed Mama's portrait on the cloth-covered bedside table, Marie-Grace heard the steamboat's whistle pierce the air. Then the *Liberty* lurched forward.

Marie-Grace hurried to the window to watch the boat pull away from the levee. "We're on our way!" she announced. She turned to Wilhelmina. "Do you think—" she started to ask. But then she stopped. Wilhelmina had curled up on the bed and was sound asleep. Her mouth was open and she was snoring gently. *I guess she was tired after all*, thought Marie-Grace.

Clang, clang! Marie-Grace jumped at the

sound of the bell outside her stateroom. A waiter called loudly in an Irish accent, "Supper will be served in ten minutes!"

Thank goodness! thought Marie-Grace. She put down the book she had been reading by the light of the oil lamp. For the last hour or so, she'd smelled delicious aromas of meat roasting and bread baking. Now she was hungry and glad to see that Wilhelmina's eyes were finally open.

"What's that noise?" Wilhelmina asked, sitting up quickly.

"It's the bell for supper. You've been asleep for a while," said Marie-Grace. She didn't mention that during the long afternoon, the steamboat had stopped once to bring aboard wood and another time to let a passenger off at a plantation. Crewmen had brought Wilhelmina's smaller trunk into the stateroom, and Papa, Sister Catherine, and Sister Frederica had also stopped by to see if Wilhelmina was all right. Annabelle had poked her head in several times, too. Wilhelmina had slept soundly through all the comings and goings.

As Wilhelmina stood up, her foot banged against her brass-bound trunk. It was so close to Marie-Grace's trunk that there was barely room to move.

"Where's the other trunk?" Wilhelmina asked. She looked confused. "The big one?"

"It's down on the main deck, with the rest of the cargo," Marie-Grace reminded her. "Captain Smith promised that it'd be safe there."

"People shouldn't make promises that they can't keep!" declared Wilhelmina, frowning. She bent over her trunk and checked its lock. "You didn't open it, did you?"

"No, of course not," said Marie-Grace, surprised by the question.

Outside the stateroom, the bell rang again. "Supper is served!" called the waiter.

Marie-Grace wrapped her gray wool shawl around her shoulders. "We'd better go," she said, edging her way past the trunks.

"I don't want to," Wilhelmina replied, sinking back down onto the bed.

Marie-Grace paused by the door, uncertain

what to do. *Papa said that Wilhelmina needs to eat*, she thought. Then she remembered that Wilhelmina had traveled downriver as a deck passenger. Those passengers had to either bring their own food or buy meals from the steamboat's kitchen. *Maybe Wilhelmina thinks she has to pay for her food*, thought Marie-Grace. *But she doesn't have any money.*

"Well," said Marie-Grace, resting her hand on the doorknob, "I wouldn't want to miss supper, 'cause I know we can eat in the main cabin. We can have as much as we want, too."

Wilhelmina's eyebrows rose. "Really?"

"Yes," Marie-Grace assured her. "You're a cabin passenger, so you don't have to pay anything extra for meals."

"I guess I might as well go, then," said Wilhelmina, jumping up. Together, the two girls walked into the main cabin. The room stretched almost the full length of the steamboat. Crystal chandeliers hung from the high ceiling. Their lights glimmered on the gold-trimmed walls and were reflected in huge gilt-framed mirrors.

"Gracious!" murmered Wilhelmina as she looked around the elegant room. "I've never seen anything so fancy in all my life."

"It is pretty," agreed Marie-Grace, smiling as she led the way through the main cabin. The back of the room was set aside as the ladies' sitting area. It looked like a fashionable parlor, with a grand piano, velvet-covered sofas, and fine carpets. The forward part of the cabin was designed for gentlemen passengers. It had polished wood floors instead of carpets, and it was furnished with mahogany tables and chairs. During most of the day, the gentlemen's area was filled with men playing cards.

Now that it was mealtime, the tables in the center of the room were covered with white linens and set with bowls and platters of food. There were a dozen passengers at each table, and the room was humming with conversation.

Marie-Grace saw Mrs. Rumsford and Annabelle at the far end of the room, and she waved to them. Then she and Wilhelmina joined the table where Papa was sitting with

Sister Catherine and Sister Frederica. Papa had saved two chairs for the girls, and they sat down just as the other passengers at the table were introducing themselves.

Marie-Grace recognized Mr. Zachariah Hopkins as the man with glasses whom she had almost run into earlier. His blond hair was slicked back neatly and parted in the middle, and his white shirt was freshly pressed.

"I recently finished school in Virginia," said Mr. Hopkins as he helped himself to roast chicken. "I've always wanted to see the Mississippi River, and I thought a ride on the *Liberty* would be a grand experience."

Sister Catherine studied his face. "You've been to New Orleans before though, haven't you?" she asked.

"No, ma'am," Mr. Hopkins replied with a smile. "My family is from Virginia, and I attended the College of William and Mary there."

"How peculiar!" said Sister Catherine. "You look so much like a young man who visited our hospital during the yellow fever epidemic last summer. That young man did not wear spectacles, though."

"Well, I've had to wear eyeglasses since I was a little boy," said Mr. Hopkins as he pushed the wire frames back up on the bridge of his nose.

The painter Marie-Grace had seen on the deck was at the table, too. He was a dark-haired young man with sad-looking brown eyes, and he spoke English with a French accent.

"My name is Jacques Paul André," he said. He gave a little bow to the table and explained that he had traveled all the way from Paris so that he could paint pictures of America.

"If anyone would like to have a portrait painted during this trip, I will be happy to oblige." He smiled and then added, "For a small fee, of course."

"Oh, I'd love to have my portrait painted!" said the plump, middle-aged woman that Marie-Grace had seen on deck when Wilhelmina first came on board. Now the woman and her husband, a bald man who was equally plump, introduced themselves as Mr. and Mrs. Reginald

Montjoy. They said that they were on their way
to perform at a theater in Chicago.

"Reggie and I travel all over the country,"
said Mrs. Montjoy, whose red-rouged cheeks
looked like bright apples against her pale skin.
"We do theater, magic, music—almost every
kind of show."

Mr. Montjoy looked up from his plate of
venison, fish, and potatoes. "We're known as the
Magnificent Montjoys," he said proudly. "Captain
Smith has asked us to put on a magic show
tomorrow night, and all the cabin passengers will
be invited."

How exciting! thought Marie-Grace. She
loved music and theater, and she had never
seen a magic show before. She looked over at
Wilhelmina, but the girl was so busy eating
that she didn't even glance up.

Marie-Grace reached for the gravy bowl.
There was only about a teaspoon of gravy left,
and she dribbled it onto her potatoes. A moment
later, a tall, heavyset man with a mustache settled
himself in the last available chair at the table, just

across from Marie-Grace.

The man looked at the empty gravy bowl and frowned. "Waiter!" he boomed. "Bring us some more gravy and be quick about it." Then he nodded to the table. "Hello, everyone. I'm Jack Bold. I sell jewelry up and down the Mississippi River. Wedding rings, watches, ladies' lockets—anything you need, I'm your man." He smiled broadly. "Glad to meet you all!"

While the others at the table greeted Mr. Bold, Wilhelmina dropped her fork and stared at him. "I remember you from Monsieur LaPlante's hotel!" she said accusingly.

"Yes, I was there—what a coincidence to see you here now," said Mr. Bold, looking surprised. "I am very sorry about your loss." He paused, and then asked, "Tell me, did you ever find what you were, ah, looking for?"

"Not yet," said Wilhelmina. She glared at him, and then she picked up her fork and bent over her food again.

What was Wilhelmina looking for? Marie-Grace wondered. *And why is she angry at this man?*

Marie-Grace helped herself to crispy fish covered with a creamy sauce. The sauce was delicious, and Marie-Grace saw that Wilhelmina was eating it hungrily, too. "It's good, isn't it?" Marie-Grace whispered.

Wilhelmina glanced up, nodded, and then looked down at her plate again. When a waiter brought several pies and cakes to the table, Wilhelmina finished her fish and helped herself to a generous slice of pecan pie. She ate every morsel of the pie, and then she slipped away from the table without a word.

Marie-Grace's heart sank as Wilhelmina hurried out of the main cabin. *She doesn't want to talk to me at all*, thought Marie-Grace.

As soon as Wilhelmina was out of sight, Mr. Bold shook his head. "That poor girl!" he said with a sigh. "When I was at LaPlante's hotel, I heard that her father had found a small fortune in gold out in California. Mr. Newman was bringing the gold back home when he got sick, and he died at the hotel while I was staying there. It was a terrible thing."

"That's a shame," said Mr. Montjoy sympathetically. His bald head shone in the chandeliers' light. "But at least his daughter got the gold."

"I'm afraid not," said Mr. Bold. He took a sip of his coffee. "After Newman died, his daughter arrived. She searched all through her father's things, but she says she didn't find any gold."

"Could Monsieur LaPlante have taken the gold himself—before Wilhelmina got there?" Mr. Hopkins asked. He pushed his eyeglasses up on his nose. "Innkeepers can't always be trusted."

Papa spoke up. "I have heard of Monsieur LaPlante. He is well respected in New Orleans," he said. "He's known for being an honest man, and a good innkeeper, too."

"Yes, that's why I stayed at his hotel," agreed Mr. Bold. "I don't believe old LaPlante would take anything that didn't belong to him. Still, no one knows what happened to the gold. Everyone at the inn was talking about the mystery."

"Why didn't Wilhelmina's father leave a note saying what he'd done with the gold?" asked

Mrs. Montjoy. She looked concerned. "That would've been the sensible thing to do."

"Well, you're right, ma'am," said Mr. Bold. He helped himself to another piece of pie. "And maybe he would have if he'd been well enough. But he was very sick. All I heard him talk about were fairy tales and nursery rhymes, and none of it made any sense."

Monsieur André looked up from his plate. "Then the gold is still hidden somewhere?" he asked, suddenly interested.

Mr. Bold took a bite of pie. "I suppose it could be," he agreed, chewing thoughtfully. "But LaPlante said that all Newman left behind was his two trunks. So if he hid the gold, I guess it would have to be in those trunks."

Marie-Grace remembered how worried Wilhelmina had been about the trunks. *I guess that's why,* she thought.

"Perhaps Mr. Newman buried the gold!" Mrs. Montjoy suggested. She leaned forward, her eyes shining with excitement. "He might've left a secret map that shows were the gold is hidden.

That's what pirates used to do!"

"I don't know about that, ma'am," Mr. Bold said doubtfully. "But I hope the gold isn't lost. From what I've heard, Wilhelmina's family is as poor as church mice." Mr. Bold shook his head. "It'd be a shame if the child couldn't find the fortune that her father worked so hard to get."

"We'll say a prayer for the girl," said Sister Catherine. Sister Frederica nodded.

No wonder Wilhelmina is so upset, thought Marie-Grace. *Her father died trying to bring back gold from California—and now the gold is missing!*

3

A WARNING

After the meal, there were scraping sounds as chairs were pushed away from the tables throughout the large main cabin. "Gentlemen, I think it's time to play cards," announced Mr. Bold. He looked around the table. "You'll join me, won't you?"

Mr. Montjoy and Monsieur André quickly agreed, but Mr. Hopkins hesitated. "I used to lose money when I played cards in college," he said. He lowered his voice. "Besides, I've heard that you have to watch out for gamblers and thieves on steamboats."

Are there really thieves on board? Marie-Grace wondered. There was a sign in the gentlemen's area that warned:

A WARNING

All card playing is at your own risk.
Passengers are strongly advised not to gamble.

But Mr. Bold didn't seem concerned. He slapped Mr. Hopkins on the back. "Don't worry, young man, this is just a friendly game of cards. Perhaps your luck has changed."

"Perhaps," said Mr. Hopkins doubtfully. "But I think I'd better read instead."

Mr. Bold turned to Marie-Grace's father. "How about you, Doctor? You'll join us, won't you?"

"Thank you, but not tonight," said Papa. He smiled at Marie-Grace. "Mr. Stevenson has invited us to see the pilothouse."

"It's beautiful up here!" exclaimed Marie-Grace, looking out the wide window. The pilothouse was a small room, set like a cabin at the very top of the steamboat. From its open windows, Marie-Grace could see the moon shining on the water. It made a glittering path across the dark Mississippi. Marie-Grace had been in a pilothouse once before, on Uncle Luc's steamboat, but she had never seen the river on a night like this.

"It is indeed a beautiful view," agreed Papa. "Marie-Grace and I appreciate your inviting us up here, Mr. Stevenson."

"Well, it's an honor to have you aboard the *Liberty*, sir," said Mr. Stevenson as he stood at the huge wooden wheel that steered the boat. He spoke in a slow drawl, as if he had all the time in the world. "I'll never forget how you saved my son when he was so sick with yellow fever, Dr. Gardner. If there's anything I can do for you during the voyage, anything at all, please let me know."

Marie-Grace saw a light on the river. "What's that?" she asked, peering into the darkness.

"That's another steamboat—it's traveling downriver," said Mr. Stevenson, shifting the wheel slightly. "All the boats are supposed to have lights burning at night, but some of them, especially the rafts, are hard to see."

Marie-Grace saw other lights twinkling in the distance. "Are there a lot of boats on the river tonight?" she asked.

"Yes, indeed," said Mr. Stevenson. "In fact, I think I'll tell the crew in the engine room to cut back on our speed." He reached up and pulled a cord overhead. A shrill bell rang out.

"Can they hear that all the way down in the engine room?" asked Marie-Grace. She leaned forward, studying the bellpulls and machinery near the wheel.

"Yes," said Mr. Stevenson as he shifted the wheel. "We even have a speaking tube. If I ring the attention bell, they know to listen." Mr. Stevenson tugged on a bellpull and then spoke loudly into a metal tube near the wheel. "Quarter speed!" he announced.

"Quarter speed!" a man's voice called back from the engine room.

"They can call up here, too," Mr. Stevenson explained.

"That's impressive," said Papa, who was

standing by the stove at the back of the pilothouse. "I wish I had a speaking tube like that at home. I could call upstairs without even leaving my office."

Wouldn't that be handy, thought Marie-Grace, smiling at the very idea.

A black-and-white cat stalked into the room, and Mr. Stevenson introduced her as Cleopatra, the pilothouse's cat. Cleopatra went straight to Marie-Grace and sat by her feet.

"Hello!" said Marie-Grace delightedly. She bent down and scratched Cleopatra's ear. The cat purred and rubbed up against her.

As Marie-Grace stroked Cleopatra's silky fur, Mr. Stevenson talked about the river. His gaze seemed to penetrate the night's blackness, and he pointed out a log that was almost completely underwater.

"That's called a snag," Mr. Stevenson explained. "We have to watch out for logs and tree trunks. If we hit them, snags can damage the boat, and we sure don't want that."

Marie-Grace looked out into the darkness.

She had heard stories about steamboats sinking
in the river or running aground, and she knew
that there were other hazards, too. Fires spread
quickly through the wooden boats, and there
could be terrible accidents if the powerful
engines exploded.

Despite the possible dangers in the river,
Mr. Stevenson seemed as relaxed as if he were
steering a carriage on a bright summer morning.
He rang the bells again, and the steamboat began
to pick up speed. "I hope you'll enjoy your trip
on the *Liberty*," said the pilot as he shifted the
huge wheel. "I think you'll like the passengers.
You meet all kinds of people on a steamboat, and
most are the nicest folks you could ever want to
know."

Marie-Grace remembered what Mr. Hopkins
had said. "Is it true that you have to watch out for
gamblers and thieves?" she asked the pilot.

Mr. Stevenson peered out the window for
a moment before answering. "Sometimes we
get some bad 'uns, I'm afraid," he admitted.
"But if anyone causes problems, the captain'll

take care of them." The wheel creaked as Mr. Stevenson turned it again. "Don't you worry, Miss Marie-Grace."

"Yes, sir," said Marie-Grace. But as she looked out at the river ahead, she wondered about Wilhelmina. The red-haired girl seemed very unhappy, and Marie-Grace was beginning to understand why. *I'll talk to Wilhelmina when I get back to the room,* Marie-Grace decided. *Maybe there's something I can do to help.*

When Marie-Grace returned to her room, however, Wilhelmina wasn't there. *Is she taking a walk?* Marie-Grace wondered.

Marie-Grace opened the door that led outside. She didn't see anyone, and the shadowy gallery looked eerie at night. She shut the door and sat uneasily on the lower berth. The minutes ticked by, but Wilhelmina still did not return.

Suddenly, she heard a man yell, "Ow! She kicked me!"

A WARNING

"Let me go!" cried Wilhelmina.

Marie-Grace sprang to the gallery door. When she opened it, she couldn't see anyone, but she heard Captain Smith's commanding voice. "Let her go, Jenkins," he ordered. "As for you, young lady, you're not allowed to go down to the main deck by yourself again. You could fall overboard, and no one would even know you were gone."

"I wanted to check my trunk!" protested Wilhelmina.

"Your trunk is safe," said the captain firmly. "And if you cause any more problems, I'll put you on shore at the next landing. Do you understand?"

A moment later, Wilhelmina flew into the stateroom, slamming the door behind her. She sat down on the bottom berth, her head sunk in her hands.

Marie-Grace was afraid that she might be crying. She pulled out her handkerchief and handed it to Wilhelmina. "What's wrong?"

When Wilhelmina looked up, her eyes weren't filled with tears—they were burning with anger.

"Everything! I'm so mad I could spit." Ignoring the handkerchief in her lap, she folded her thin arms across her chest. "I'd just found my father's trunk when that deckhand saw me. He said I wasn't allowed on the main deck. Then he dragged me up to see the captain." She let out a frustrated sigh. "I wish I'd kicked him harder!"

"Why do you want the other trunk?" asked Marie-Grace. "If you need clothes, you can borrow some of mine." She nodded toward her own trunk.

Wilhelmina set her mouth in a determined line. "I don't care about clothes. My father gave me something, and I have to get it."

"I'm very sorry about your father," said Marie-Grace quietly. "I know how hard it is to lose someone you love."

"You can't know," Wilhelmina replied. "*Your* father is here with you."

Marie-Grace hesitated for a moment. Then she picked up the framed portrait from the bedside table. "This is my mother," she said, showing the picture to Wilhelmina. "She and my baby brother, Daniel, died when I was five years old."

For a few moments, the only noise in the tiny stateroom was the pounding of the steamboat's engines. "Well, maybe you *would* understand then," Wilhelmina said at last. She picked up Marie-Grace's handkerchief and twisted it tightly in her hands. Then she said slowly, "I have to find my father's gold. Will you help me?"

Wilhelmina looked so worried that Marie-Grace felt her own stomach tighten. But she nodded. "I'll help if I can," she said. "Tell me what happened."

"It started when my pa went off to the Gold Rush," Wilhelmina began. She settled back on her bed and wrapped her arms around her knees. "That was about four years ago. Pa wanted us to have a farm of our own, but we didn't have enough money. So Pa decided to go out west and find gold. He promised me and my little brothers, Johnny and Ned, that he'd come home soon with enough money to buy us a piece of land. We thought we'd have our own farm by spring."

Wilhelmina paused and then shook her head.

"We were wrong," she said, staring down at the wood floor. "Two years after Pa left, my ma died of a fever. Grammy's been taking care of us ever since. She used to earn money by sewing for our neighbors, but she can't see as good as she used to. Now I take in sewing, but we never have enough money." She looked up at Marie-Grace. "Sometimes we don't have enough food, either."

Marie-Grace drew in her breath. There had been times when her father hadn't had much money, but they had always had enough to eat. *It must be awfully hard to be hungry,* she thought.

"We have cousins in Kansas," Wilhelmina continued. "They wrote and offered to take in Johnny and Ned. They said they could use help on their farm and that they'd raise the boys as if they were their own sons." Wilhelmina sighed heavily. "Our family would be split apart. We didn't want that to happen, but we didn't have any other choice."

Marie-Grace nodded sympathetically. She had seen parents leave their children at the Holy Trinity Orphanage because they had no way to care for them. She knew it was a heart-wrenching decision. "What did you do?" Marie-Grace asked.

"Well, before we had to decide, we got a letter from Pa," Wilhelmina continued. "He said he'd finally found gold, and he was going to bring it home to us as fast as he could."

Wilhelmina explained that instead of taking a wagon across the country, her father had decided that he could save time by taking a ship from California to Panama. He'd crossed the Isthmus of Panama on horseback and then boarded a different ship to New Orleans. Somewhere along the journey, he'd come down with a fever.

By the time her father had reached New Orleans, he'd known he was very sick. He'd sent a telegram, telling Wilhelmina to come at once to meet him. But Wilhelmina hadn't been able to leave right away.

"Grammy couldn't go with me, and she wouldn't let me go by myself. She didn't want me to get lost. I had to wait two days until someone we knew could travel with me," Wilhelmina recalled. She hugged her knees tighter and, in a choked voice, said, "Pa passed away before I got to New Orleans."

Marie-Grace gently touched Wilhelmina's arm. "I'm so sorry."

After a pause, Wilhelmina said, "When I got to the hotel, Monsieur LaPlante was kind to me. He'd guarded Pa's trunks, and he gave me the keys in an envelope fastened with sealing wax— just the way Pa left them for me. There was a note with the keys, too."

Wilhelmina reached inside her pocket and pulled out a folded piece of paper. She handed it to Marie-Grace, who opened it and read the shaky writing:

My dearest Wilhelmina,

If I am gone before you arrive, Monsieur LaPlante will give you my trunks to take home with you. Monsieur LaPlante is a good man, but I have not told even him where the gold is hidden. I dare not tell you now in case this note falls into the wrong hands. But do not doubt that I have kept the promise I made to you and your brothers.

A Warning

Do you remember the riddles I used to send you?
I have prepared one last riddle for you. I meant to
surprise you with it when I arrived home, but now
I must ask you to solve the riddle on your own.
With love,
Pa

Marie-Grace looked up. "Where's the riddle?"

"I haven't found it yet, but I think it's in the book Pa left me," Wilhelmina said. "The book is in the other trunk, and I *have* to get it." She stood up. "Will you come with me to the main deck?"

Marie-Grace swallowed hard. "Captain Smith said you're not allowed to go back down there," she reminded Wilhelmina. "You could get into trouble."

"He said I wasn't supposed to go there *alone*," Wilhelmina corrected her. "But if you come with me, I won't be alone. And you could watch to make sure no one sees us."

"I don't know," Marie-Grace hesitated.

"It won't take long," Wilhelmina pleaded. "I promise."

THE HIDDEN GOLD

Marie-Grace glanced around the room. Her mother's portrait seemed to be looking back at her. *I wanted to help her, and this is my chance,* thought Marie-Grace. "All right," she said, standing up.

For the first time since she'd come aboard the *Liberty*, Wilhelmina smiled. "Thank you."

4

RIDDLES AND RHYMES

Wilhelmina opened the door and peered out into the gallery. She motioned to Marie-Grace. "Come on!"

The girls hurried along the narrow gallery, past the starboard paddle wheel, and toward the steep steps at the front of the steamboat. Marie-Grace's palms were sweating. She knew that deck passengers were forbidden to come up the stairs to the more expensive cabin areas. But she wasn't sure what the rules were about stateroom passengers going downstairs.

On the main deck, Wilhelmina led the way past piles of cargo. Marie-Grace could smell cabbage stewing, and she heard people talking in languages she didn't understand. But she didn't see any crew members.

As they slipped along the shadows, Marie-Grace glanced out over the river. From the pilothouse the dark water had looked beautiful, but now that it was so close, it was frightening. There was no guardrail, and the deck was only inches above the river. Marie-Grace shuddered to herself as she remembered the captain's warning to Wilhelmina: "You could fall overboard and no one would even know you were gone." Now Marie-Grace watched her step carefully on the slippery deck and tried to keep as far away as she could from the edge.

Just before the girls reached the engine room, Wilhelmina stopped short. Marie-Grace saw a faint light seeping from the cracks around closed door, and she felt the deck tremble with the pounding of the steam engines. Marie-Grace heard a man on the other side of the door shouting something, but she couldn't make out the words.

After a few moments, Wilhelmina tugged on Marie-Grace's arm. "This way," she whispered.

Wilhelmina turned into a walkway that

stretched from one side of the steamboat to the other. Boxes, barrels, sacks, and crates lined both sides of the passage, and the dim light from the engine room cast shadows on the narrow aisle.

Marie-Grace felt an uncomfortable tingling at the back of her neck, as if someone were watching her. But when she turned around, no one was there. "Where are we going?" Marie-Grace whispered.

Wilhelmina gestured toward a huge crate and some barrels farther down the walkway. "Over there," she whispered back.

The girls had almost reached the center of the passage when they heard laughter nearby. Both girls ducked behind the big crate. Peeking out to the side, Marie-Grace saw two men strolling along the port side of the steamboat. She held her breath as they walked past, hoping they wouldn't notice her or Wilhelmina. But neither man looked in the girls' direction. For a moment there was a gleam of light, and then a door slammed shut. Marie-Grace guessed that the two men had gone into the engine room. "Thank heavens they didn't come this way," she whispered.

Wilhelmina nodded. She ventured a few steps farther down the passageway and stopped in front of a big trunk. She took a key from her pocket, fumbled with the lock for a moment, and opened the trunk. Then she began pulling out thick blankets.

"What are you doing?" asked Marie-Grace.

"I have to get to the bottom of the trunk," Wilhelmina explained. "That's where I hid the book." She piled several blankets on top of the barrels and then reached in the trunk again.

"Here's my father's shovel," Wilhelmina said. "And his gold pan . . ."

"A pan made of real gold?" Marie-Grace asked. She leaned forward to get a better look in the dim light.

"No, a pan used to sort gold from rocks," Wilhelmina said, as if everyone should know what a gold pan is. "Miners always have them."

"Oh," said Marie-Grace, disappointed.

Wilhelmina grunted with effort as she pulled out a bucket, a coffeepot, and a black pot with three short legs attached to it.

"What's that?" whispered Marie-Grace.

"It's a spider—it sits on its legs in the cook fire," Wilhelmina whispered back. "Don't you have one? I cook beans in ours at home."

"I don't cook much," Marie-Grace admitted.

"What *do* you do?" whispered Wilhelmina.

"Well," said Marie-Grace, "I go to school and take singing lessons. I help my father in his office sometimes, and I help our housekeeper, too."

"You take singing lessons *and* you have a housekeeper—you do have an easy life!" whispered Wilhelmina in the darkness.

Marie-Grace thought of her friend Cécile, whose family had a cook and other servants. *What would Wilhelmina think of Cécile's life?* she wondered.

Wilhelmina quickly pulled out a big spoon, and a tin mug. Then she dragged out a thick black skillet. "This is a frying pan. Pa made flapjacks on our frying pan at home."

"I know what a frying pan is!" Marie-Grace whispered back. She was annoyed that

Wilhelmina seemed to think that she had a life of luxury. "I help with cooking *sometimes*. And we'd better hurry before someone finds us."

Wilhelmina ran her hand around the nearly empty trunk and pulled out a small book. "Here's what I need," she said triumphantly. "Hold it for me, will you?"

Marie-Grace squinted at the thin cloth-covered volume. "*This* is what your father left you?" she asked with surprise.

"Yes," said Wilhelmina as she piled the things back into the trunk. "And I think it's very important."

5
CLUES IN THE PAGES

As soon as Wilhelmina locked the trunk, she took the book from Marie-Grace. "Let's go," she whispered.

The girls made their way back through the maze of cargo and sleeping passengers on the main deck as quietly as they could. Then they ran up the stairs to the boiler deck and hurried to their stateroom. Marie-Grace bolted the door behind them while Wilhelmina sunk down on her bed and opened the cloth-covered volume.

Marie-Grace looked at the title with curiosity. "Why did your father have a book of nursery rhymes with him?" she asked.

"Pa gave me this when I was little. He used to read to me from it me every night," Wilhelmina explained. "When he left for California, I put the book in his trunk as a surprise. I wanted him to read it and think about me, even when he was far away."

Wilhelmina leafed through the book's yellowed pages. "I know that Pa did read it, because sometimes he'd send me letters with riddles about the nursery rhymes. At first they were easy riddles. One time he wrote, 'In the storm, my tent was like a bridge in London. Can you guess how?'"

"It was falling down?" ventured Marie-Grace.

"That's right," said Wilhelmina. "Pa didn't send riddles with every letter, just once in a while. He hadn't sent any in a long time, and I'd started to think he'd forgotten about them."

"But he hadn't," Marie-Grace guessed. She sat down on the berth beside Wilhelmina. "That's why he wrote about the riddles in his letter?"

Wilhelmina nodded. "When I got to New Orleans, Monsieur LaPlante said that Pa had only talked foolishness, saying things like "cats and crowns and London Bridge."

"London Bridge?" Marie-Grace asked.

"Yes," said Wilhelmina. "That's when I knew that Pa hadn't been talking foolishness at all. He was talking about the nursery rhymes! I guess Monsieur LaPlante didn't understand them because he's French."

For a moment, Wilhelmina stared down at the book in her hands. "I think Pa left me clues about where to look for the gold. In his note he said I should solve the riddle, so he was depending on me to understand what he meant." She looked up at Marie-Grace. "The trouble is, I don't understand."

Marie-Grace didn't understand, either. "Why would your father hide the gold? Why didn't he just put it in the trunk and lock it up?"

"Pa had gold stolen from him once, when he first started mining in California," Wilhelmina said. "So he was very careful." She frowned. "I'm sure he hid the gold somewhere, but I've looked all through the book, and I don't know which riddles are clues."

"Would you like me to look?" Marie-Grace offered. "Maybe I'll see something you missed."

THE HIDDEN GOLD

Wilhelmina hesitated for a moment, but then she handed the book to Marie-Grace.

The faded cloth cover was worn smooth. By the dim light of the oil lamp, Marie-Grace carefully turned the pages. There was the London Bridge rhyme:

> *London Bridge has fallen down,*
> *Has fallen down, has fallen down.*
> *London Bridge has fallen down,*
> *My fair lady.*

Marie-Grace shivered at the next lines.

> *Build it up with silver and gold,*
> *Silver and gold, silver and gold,*
> *Build it up with silver and gold,*
> *My fair lady.*
>
> *Silver and gold will be stolen away,*
> *Stolen away, stolen away,*
> *Silver and gold will be stolen away,*
> *My fair lady.*

Marie-Grace turned to Wilhelmina. "Look at this," she said, pointing to the last verse. "Could someone have stolen the gold even though your pa tried to hide it? It might've happened when he was sick."

"I don't think so," said Wilhelmina, shaking her head. "Pa said that he hadn't forgotten his promise, so I'm sure he still had the gold when he got to New Orleans. And Monsieur LaPlante kept the keys safe, just like he'd said he would."

Marie-Grace carefully read the rest of the rhymes, and then she handed the book back to Wilhelmina. "I'm sorry," she said reluctantly. "I don't see anything that looks like a clue."

Wilhelmina brushed her red hair back from her forehead. "The gold has to be somewhere— it just has to be!"

Marie-Grace was tired from the long day, but Wilhelmina looked so miserable that she said, "We could search *this* trunk again, if you'd like." She pointed to the brass-bound trunk at her feet.

"I *was* awfully tired at the hotel," said Wilhelmina, a glimmer of hope reappearing in her eyes. "I guess I could've missed something." She unlocked the trunk and began taking things out, feeling each item carefully as she picked it up. "Gold is heavy, so if Pa did hide it somewhere, we should be able to feel it—even if we can't see it," she explained to Marie-Grace.

Marie-Grace looked closely at the sturdy work clothes, thick wool socks, and well-worn boots that Wilhelmina pulled from the trunk. Nothing seemed unusually heavy until she picked up a folded flannel shirt and felt something solid. Excited, she unfolded the shirt. There was a framed portrait of a little girl holding hands with a much smaller boy.

Wilhelmina glanced over Marie-Grace's shoulder. "That's me and my brother Johnny, when we were little. Ned wasn't born yet. I put it inside the shirt so the frame wouldn't break."

Marie-Grace turned the picture over, wondering if anything might be behind it. "Did you open the frame?"

"Our names are on the back of the portrait, that's all," said Wilhelmina, and she carefully folded the shirt around the frame again.

Marie-Grace kept looking through the items. At the bottom of the trunk, she saw a violin case. "Did your pa play music?"

"Yes," said Wilhelmina. She touched the violin case tenderly. "Pa knew how to do lots of things. He was a carpenter, and a blacksmith, and a good farmer, too."

The trunk was empty now. The girls examined the wood inside the trunk, but they didn't find any hidden clues.

"Pa wanted more than anything for us to have our own farm," Wilhelmina said quietly. "He was always talking about it in his letters. He said we'd have cows and chickens and a big garden." She began folding the clothes again. "He was so excited that he'd finally found enough gold to buy some land."

As Marie-Grace helped Wilhelmina put everything back into the trunk, she asked, "Do you think your pa might have changed the gold into paper money—or something else that might've been easier to hide?"

"He always said he'd bring home gold," Wilhelmina replied. "He might have changed his mind, but I doubt it. Paper money is too easy to steal." Wilhelmina locked the trunk and pocketed the key. Then she set her shoulders with determination. "Let's look through the nursery rhymes again," she urged Marie-Grace. "There must be a clue somewhere in the book."

Marie-Grace tried to fight back a yawn. "I have to get ready for bed first," she told Wilhelmina. "I'll be back soon, and then I'll help you look."

But by the time Marie-Grace returned from the washroom, Wilhelmina had fallen asleep on the lower berth. She was still fully dressed, and the book of nursery rhymes lay open next to her.

Marie-Grace pulled a blanket over Wilhelmina. Then she picked up the book and leafed through it again. This time she noticed that the corner of one of the pages was turned down. On the left-hand page was a picture of a boy and a girl walking up a hill, carrying a pail between them. Beneath the picture were two rhymes:

Jack and Jill
Went up the hill
To fetch a pail of water;
Jack fell down,
And cracked his crown,
And Jill came tumbling after.

Hey diddle diddle,
The cat and the fiddle,
The cow jumped over the moon;
The little dog laughed
To see such fine sport,
And the dish ran after the spoon.

The right-hand side had a picture of a little girl with a round face and a head full of curls. She was sitting on a chair, and her eyes were wide with surprise. Below the picture were two more rhymes:

Little Miss Muffet
She sat on a tuffet,
Eating of curds and whey;
There came a little spider,
Who sat down beside her,
And frightened Miss Muffet away.

THE HIDDEN GOLD

Little Jack Horner
Sat in a corner
Eating a Christmas pie;
He put in his thumb
And pull'd out a plum,
And said "What a good boy am I!"

Marie-Grace stared at the pages for a few moments. Then she put the book on the bedside table and blew out the lamp. *I'll look at the pages again tomorrow,* she told herself as she climbed up to the top berth. *Maybe together Wilhelmina and I can find a clue.*

6
PANIC AT NIGHT

The rhythmic splashing of the steamboat's paddle wheels rocked Marie-Grace into a sound sleep. But she was awakened before dawn by the sound of her father's voice.

"Wait!" he was shouting from not too far away. "I'll get my bag and be there in a moment!"

Marie-Grace bolted up in bed. The steamboat had stopped—the powerful engines were no longer thudding. She knew it wasn't just a routine stop because she could hear people yelling for help. Her stomach twisted with fear. Had there been an accident?

As Marie-Grace climbed down from the upper berth, she hit her foot on Wilhelmina's trunk. For a moment, she'd forgotten all about Wilhelmina. Now she realized that, if the steamboat was sinking, they would both have to be ready to escape.

"Wake up!" she cried, shaking Wilhelmina's shoulder. "Something's wrong."

Wilhelmina stumbled out of bed, still dressed from the night before. Marie-Grace threw a shawl around her shoulders, and the girls rushed out to the deck together. Other passengers had already gathered outside, and men with lanterns were running and shouting. Marie-Grace saw Monsieur André, who looked half-asleep, and Mr. and Mrs. Montjoy, who were both wearing nightcaps. Mrs. Rumsford came on deck carrying her baby, who was crying loudly, and Annabelle followed closely behind her mother.

Mr. Bold arrived a few moments later. "What's wrong?" he demanded. "Why have we stopped?"

"Those men on the shore are hurt, and the boat's stopped to help them," someone said. "See, the doctor is with them."

Marie-Grace, Wilhelmina, and the others gathered by the railing to watch what was happening. The sun was beginning to rise, and by its light, Marie-Grace could see her father on the nearby shore. The nuns were with him, along with several men holding lanterns. Marie-Grace was leaning out over the railing, watching the shore, when she felt a tug at her skirt.

"Marie-Grace, let's feed the gulls."

Marie-Grace glanced down. Annabelle was holding her doll and looking at Marie-Grace hopefully. "No, Annabelle, not now." The little girl's face fell, and Marie-Grace added, "The birds are still sleeping. But we can play another time."

As Annabelle turned away, Marie-Grace saw Mr. Stevenson standing by the railing. She and Wilhelmina hurried over to him.

"Don't worry—your father's all right," he assured Marie-Grace. "But there was an accident. Another steamboat hit a flatboat going downriver. The flatboat crew was hurt pretty bad, but the steamboat didn't see 'em and just kept going."

"Oh, that's awful!" Wilhelmina declared.

"Yes," the pilot agreed. "Luckily the men

made it to shore, though, and we saw their signal from the pilothouse." Mr. Stevenson looked toward the main deck, where there was a flurry of activity. "They're bringing them aboard now. I'll help. You girls stay here."

There was noise, shouting, and confusion everywhere. From the railing of the upper deck, Marie-Grace and Wilhelmina watched a small boat crammed with people row up to the side of the *Liberty.* The deck was lit by men holding lanterns, and Marie-Grace saw her father help the patients on board. Two of the injured men were being carried on stretchers. *Those poor men!* thought Marie-Grace.

Then her eye caught a movement on the other side of the main deck. She gasped. Annabelle had somehow made her way to the deck below, and she was walking along the edge of the boat. There was nothing standing between Annabelle and the fast-flowing river.

"Oh no," cried Marie-Grace. "Annabelle!"

"What's wrong?" asked Wilhelmina.

Marie-Grace didn't have time to explain.

She tried to shout to Papa and warn him to get Annabelle away from the water, but there was too much noise for her to be heard. *Annabelle could fall in*, Marie-Grace realized with a cold, deep fear. *And the current would carry her away in a moment.*

Marie-Grace raced across the deck, dodging the other passengers. She ran as fast as she could, but the deck appeared to stretch on forever, and each step seemed painfully slow. *Oh, please, let me be in time*, she prayed silently.

Three crewmen were hurrying up the steps. Marie-Grace pushed her way past them, half stumbling, half jumping down the stairs. "Annabelle!" she cried.

Another injured man was being brought aboard on a stretcher, and no one seemed to notice Marie-Grace amid all the confusion. Marie-Grace scanned the deck for Annabelle. *Has she fallen in?* she wondered desperately. Just then, Marie-Grace saw Annabelle on a wall of crates stacked near the edge of the deck. The pile was as tall as Marie-Grace's shoulder, but Annabelle was crawling along the top as if it were a low garden wall. She didn't seem to notice how high up she was—or the swift river below her.

Marie-Grace sprinted toward her. "What are you doing, Annabelle?" She exclaimed. Marie-Grace reached up and grabbed the little girl, swinging her safely down to the deck. "You could have fallen! You should be upstairs."

"No!" cried Annabelle. She twisted away from Marie-Grace and pointed to the top of the crates. "Priscilla! My dolly! She's up there."

Marie-Grace craned her neck, but she couldn't see the doll. She stepped up onto a box. There was the doll, outlined in the soft glow of the early morning light. It was on the edge of the crate, and it looked as if it could fall into the water at any moment.

"We have to get Priscilla!" Annabelle cried.

Marie-Grace stood on her tiptoes and reached for the doll. The box she was standing on wobbled, and Marie-Grace nearly fell over.

"You'd best get down," a man said suddenly. "We've had enough accidents for one day."

Marie-Grace whirled around. For a moment she didn't recognize the man behind her. Then she realized it was Mr. Hopkins. He wasn't wearing his spectacles, and his hair, which had been so carefully slicked back at dinner, was now tousled.

"Let me get the doll," Mr. Hopkins said. He was tall, so he was able to reach the doll easily. With a bow, he handed it to Annabelle.

"Priscilla!" Annabelle exclaimed, hugging her doll tightly.

Marie-Grace thanked Mr. Hopkins. "I didn't think anyone else had seen Annabelle," she said.

"I just happened to look down at the right time," said Mr. Hopkins with a smile.

Marie-Grace kept a firm hold on Annabelle's hand as they climbed the steps to the boiler deck. Wilhelmina was still with a crowd of passengers at the railing. "Where did you go?" she asked Marie-Grace.

"I'll tell you later," Marie-Grace answered, still holding tight to Annabelle's hand. "I need to take Annabelle back to her mother."

Mrs. Rumsford had been so busy with her crying baby that she hadn't realized Annabelle was missing. When Marie-Grace explained what had happened, Mrs. Rumsford's hand flew to her mouth. "Goodness gracious!" she exclaimed. "Thank heavens you and Mr. Hopkins found her!" Then she kneeled down beside her daughter and hugged her tightly. "Annabelle, dear, don't you ever run off like that again! Ever!"

"Yes, Mama," agreed Annabelle. "And Priscilla won't, either."

As soon as Annabelle was safe, Marie-Grace began to look for Papa. She found him with the three wounded men. The patients had been carried up to the boiler deck. Papa was holding a bandage on one man's arm. Sister Catherine and Sister Frederica were helping the other patients. One of the wounded men was crying out in pain.

Marie-Grace hurried over to her father. "Can I help, Papa?"

"Yes," he said quickly. "Here, keep this in place while I check on that man."

Marie-Grace held the cloth firmly on the

man's wounded arm. "My father will be back soon," she told the patient. He nodded, his teeth clenched in pain.

The next few minutes seemed like hours to Marie-Grace. Her heart ached for the wounded man, and she was very glad when her father returned. He took Marie-Grace's place by the man's side. "Is there something else I can do, Papa?" she asked.

"Thank you, Grace, but no," Papa said as the boat's engines started up again. "We're taking the patients up to the crew's quarters. Sister Frederica and Sister Catherine are going too, so I'll have all the nurses I need. You and Wilhelmina should go back to bed."

Marie-Grace found Wilhelmina waiting for her by the deck rail. Streaks of purple and pink brightened the eastern horizon, and birds swooped in the sky, but it was not yet fully light. Marie-Grace suddenly felt very tired. "My papa doesn't need any more help," she reported. "We can go back to sleep before breakfast."

"I've taken care of my little brothers when

they've gotten hurt," said Wilhelmina as the two girls walked along the gallery. "But I've never seen anyone hurt as bad as those men were. Didn't it bother you?"

"I was scared," admitted Marie-Grace. "And I feel shaky now that it's all over."

"You didn't seem scared," said Wilhelmina. She looked at Marie-Grace with new respect. "You seemed like you knew just what to do."

"I've helped Papa before," Marie-Grace explained. She remembered all the patients who had been ill with yellow fever last summer. "I suppose I'm used to seeing sick people."

"I don't think that I could *ever* get used to that," Wilhelmina confessed. Then she frowned. "But why did you run off like that?"

As they entered their stateroom, Marie-Grace explained how she had seen Annabelle playing dangerously close to the edge of the deck.

"I'm glad you found her," said Wilhelmina. "I didn't see her at all."

"I guess Mr. Hopkins and I were the only ones," Marie-Grace replied. She shivered when she thought of how easily Annabelle could have fallen into the river.

Marie-Grace took off her shawl, climbed into the upper berth, and crawled under her blanket. She looked at her mother's picture as she always did before falling asleep. The silver-framed portrait was now facedown on the bedside table. *That's strange,* she thought, but she was too tired to get out of bed and turn over the frame. *I'll fix it later*, she promised herself.

As she drifted off to sleep, Marie-Grace thought of the silver frame and Wilhelmina's missing gold. The words of the nursery rhyme echoed in her mind with the splashing of the paddle wheels. "Silver and gold will be stolen away, stolen away, stolen away . . ."

7
MISSING

When Marie-Grace woke up, sun was
streaming into the room. She heard a noise and
looked down from her berth. Wilhelmina was
pulling the blankets and sheets off the bed below.

Marie-Grace yawned. "What are you doing?"
she asked sleepily.

"I'm looking for the book," Wilhelmina
answered. "I can't find it anywhere. Have you
seen it?"

"I put it on the table last night," Marie-Grace
said. She sat up. "It's not there anymore?"

Wilhelmina shook her head.

"Did you put it in your trunk?" asked Marie-
Grace, pointing to the brass-bound trunk in the
center of the room.

"No," said Wilhelmina. She looked close to

tears. "The trunk was locked. I opened it and checked anyway, but the book's not there."

"I'll help you look," Marie-Grace said, and she climbed down from the upper berth. Together, the girls searched the tiny stateroom. They pulled apart the sheets and blankets on both berths and even peered under the mattresses. They looked under the bedside table and behind the curtains. The small volume of nursery rhymes was nowhere to be found.

Finally, Wilhelmina sat down on the lower berth and sank her head into her hands. "It's gone! The only clue I had to the gold is gone."

Marie-Grace sat down next to her. The bedside table was so close that her knee almost touched it. Marie-Grace reached over and straightened her mother's portrait.

"When we got back to the room after the accident, I noticed that my mother's picture had fallen over," she said. "I thought it'd probably happened when the boat stopped. But your book and my picture were next to each other on the table." Marie-Grace paused and asked thoughtfully, "Do you think someone could have taken the book—and knocked the picture over at the same time?"

"Why would someone take a book of nursery rhymes and leave a silver frame behind?" Wilhelmina asked.

Marie-Grace thought for a moment. "Does anyone else know how important the book is?" she asked.

"I don't think so," Wilhelmina said, and both girls stared in silence at the pile of sheets and blankets that were now on the floor. When Wilhelmina looked up, her mouth was set in a fierce line. "Maybe Mr. Bold knew!" she exclaimed. "He was at the hotel when Pa was sick. He could have heard Pa talking about the nursery rhymes and realized they were clues. I don't trust him at all. He could have followed me on board just so he could steal the book and get to the gold!"

Marie-Grace shook her head. "You were the last person to come on board," she reminded Wilhelmina. "So Mr. Bold couldn't have followed you. He was already here."

"But he's the only one who might know about the nursery rhymes," Wilhelmina objected.

Suddenly Marie-Grace remembered the conversation at the dinner table the night before. "Oh no!" she exclaimed.

"What?"

"After you left last night, Mr. Bold told everyone about your father's gold and how it might be hidden somewhere," Marie-Grace recalled. "And he said that when your pa was sick, he talked about fairy tales and children's rhymes. So *everyone* at the table knew about the rhymes. They might have guessed that the book was important."

Wilhelmina sucked in her breath. "Who else was at the table?"

Marie-Grace closed her eyes and tried to picture the dinner table. After a moment, she opened her eyes. "I think I remember everyone," she said. She took her pen and a sheet of paper from her trunk and wrote a list:

THE HIDDEN GOLD

Papa
Sister Catherine
Sister Frederica
Mr. and Mrs. Montjoy
Mr. Hopkins
Monsieur André
Mr. Bold
Me

Wilhelmina scrunched her freckled nose. "So, anybody on this list might've taken the book?" she asked.

"Well, it wasn't me or Papa." Marie-Grace crossed out those names. "And it wasn't Sister Catherine or Sister Frederica either. Nuns wouldn't do something like that, and besides, they were with Papa." Marie-Grace crossed out the nuns' names, too.

"Mr. and Mrs. Montjoy were on deck the whole time I was there," said Wilhelmina. "Mrs. Montjoy has a loud voice, and I heard her talking, and Mr. Montjoy was right beside her."

Wilhelmina stared at the list for a moment. "I guess Monsieur André or Mr. Hopkins could have taken the book."

"Mr. Hopkins helped me with Annabelle on the main deck, but I didn't see him after that," said Marie-Grace. She thought back to the rescue. *There had been something different about Mr. Hopkins last night,* she remembered. *But what was it?*

Wilhelmina stared at her locked trunk for a few moments. "At least nothing else was taken, so I don't think the thief could have found Pa's gold," she said at last. "But without the book, I don't know how *I'm* going to find the gold."

Marie-Grace stood up. "I think we should tell Captain Smith what happened. He should know that there's a thief on board."

"No!" Wilhelmina declared. She grabbed Marie-Grace's arm. "You can't do that!"

"Why not?"

"Because when the deckhand found me by my father's trunk, I told him that all I wanted was one book. But he said he was taking me to see the captain anyway."

"Why does that matter?" asked Marie-Grace.

"If I tell the captain now that someone stole the book, he'll *know* that I went back to the main deck," Wilhelmina explained. "And the captain said he'd throw me off the boat at the next stop if I cause any more trouble. Then I'd never get home." Wilhelmina looked at Marie-Grace earnestly. "Please don't tell the captain."

Marie-Grace sank back onto the bed. "All right," she said. "But what do you think we should do?"

Before Wilhelmina could answer, a bell rang in the main cabin. "Breakfast will be served shortly," the waiter called.

Wilhelmina stood up. "We have to find the gold before anyone else does."

Breakfast had already begun by the time the girls entered the main cabin. The first thing Marie-Grace noticed was that Papa, Sister Frederica, and Sister Catherine were all absent.

They must be with the patients upstairs, she realized.

The next thing she saw was that the table was overflowing with food. There were platters of beefsteak, sliced ham, smoked fish, scrambled eggs, sausages, bread, doughnuts, and so many other foods that Marie-Grace had filled her plate before she had a chance to sample all the dishes.

"Here," said Mrs. Montjoy, holding the platter of smoked fish. "You simply must try these!" Before Marie-Grace could explain that she didn't care for any, Mrs. Montjoy plopped a tiny fish on her plate.

"Wasn't that a shocking accident this morning?" declared Mrs. Montjoy in her loud voice. "Truly terrible!"

While Wilhelmina wolfed down her breakfast, Marie-Grace examined the smoked fish on her plate. She didn't like to waste food, but the smell turned her stomach. *I know who would like it,* she thought. She slipped the fish off her plate and put it in her napkin.

As she ate, Marie-Grace watched the other passengers carefully. Most of the people were talking about the flatboat accident. Mr. Bold didn't let the food in his mouth stop him from describing the victims' wounds in gory detail. Marie-Grace noticed that he made it sound as if he'd personally saved the injured men. She was fairly sure, though, that Mr. Bold hadn't helped at all. *Does he just like to brag?* Marie-Grace wondered. *Or is he making up a story so that we won't suspect him of taking the book?*

As the other passengers discussed the events, Mr. Hopkins ate silently. Mrs. Montjoy turned to him and asked whether he thought the accident had slowed the boat so much that they'd be late for their next stop. Mr. Hopkins patted his mouth with his napkin before answering. "I don't know much about steamboats, ma'am. It appears to me, though, that we're making good time upriver now."

As Mr. Bold reached across the table for the platter of doughnuts, a seam on his shirt ripped. "Tarnation!" he exclaimed. "This is my best shirt."

Wilhelmina looked up from her plate.

"I could mend it for you," she said. "It would only cost you"—she paused—"a dime."

Mr. Bold hesitated, and then he nodded. "I'll give it to you after breakfast."

Why did Wilhelmina offer to help Mr. Bold? Marie-Grace wondered. *I thought she didn't trust him.*

As the sun poured into the main cabin, Marie-Grace looked at her fellow passengers, who all seemed so nice. *Could one of them really have stolen Wilhelmina's book?* she wondered with a chill.

8
HITTING A SNAG

After breakfast, Marie-Grace tucked her
napkin into her pocket and asked the steward
if she could take some doughnuts to her father.
The steward nodded and returned a moment
later with a basketful of warm doughnuts dusted
with sugar. "I'll bring up hot coffee soon, too,"
he promised.

"Papa, here's some breakfast," said Marie-
Grace when she arrived on the hurricane deck.
Her father and the nuns were in the crew
quarters with the patients. The wounded men
were lying on narrow cots, and two of the men
were dozing quietly. The third man, however,
was groaning in his sleep. Sister Catherine and
Sister Frederica were by the man's side.

"Is he going to be all right?" Marie-Grace

whispered to her father.

"I hope so," said Papa. He wiped his forehead with his handkerchief. "His name is Caleb. We're doing our best for him, but he's badly injured."

Marie-Grace tried to swallow the lump in her throat. She knew that sometimes patients could not be saved—no matter how hard the doctors and nurses tried. "I hope he gets better," she said quietly. She put down the basket of doughnuts. "How are the other men?"

"Fortunately, they are doing well, and I think they'll all recover," Papa said. "At the next port, Captain Smith is going to telegraph their families to meet the steamboat in New Madrid."

Marie-Grace saw that her father's jacket was stained and rumpled. She guessed that he probably hadn't slept at all. "Can I do something to help, Papa?"

"Thank you, Grace," he said. "But Sister Catherine and Sister Frederica are experienced nurses, and they are doing all that anyone can do." Papa helped himself to a doughnut. "How are you and Wilhelmina getting along?" he asked. "Is everything all right?"

Marie-Grace bit her lip. She had promised not to tell Captain Smith about the missing book, but she hadn't promised not to tell Papa. "Wilhelmina's upset because she can't find the gold her father brought back," Marie-Grace explained. "Her family's poor, and they need that gold, but she doesn't know where her father hid it. She had a book of nursery rhymes that she thinks is a clue. Now the book is missing, too."

Marie-Grace looked up at her father. "We wondered if a thief stole the book from our room so that he could find the gold," she told him. "Do you think that's possible?"

Her father took a bite of doughnut before answering. "I wouldn't be surprised if someone tried to steal Mr. Newman's gold," he said, watching Caleb from across the room. "People who are desperate for money will do all sorts of things. But steal a child's nursery rhyme book?" Papa looked back at Marie Grace and shook his head. "That doesn't seem likely."

Papa finished the doughnut and smiled wearily. "Perhaps your friend Wilhelmina just misplaced the book, but she's so upset, she *thinks* it was stolen," he suggested. "I'm sure you'll find it somewhere in your room."

Marie-Grace remembered how carefully she and Wilhelmina had searched the stateroom. *I don't think the book could be there*, she thought. But before she could say anything, Sister Frederica bustled over.

"Caleb is asking for you, Doctor Gardner," she reported.

As Papa hurried to the patient's cot, Marie-Grace slipped out of the crew quarters and climbed the steps to the pilothouse, hoping to see Mr. Stevenson. He shared duties with another pilot, and each man worked for four hours at a time. Marie-Grace was glad to see Mr. Stevenson standing at the wheel now, with Cleopatra the cat curled at his feet.

"Hello, Mr. Stevenson," Marie-Grace called.

The pilot glanced backward. "Come on in, Miss Marie-Grace. Did you go see your father?"

"Yes, sir," said Marie-Grace. She stepped inside the pilothouse to the comforting smell of coffee brewing on the stove.

"I'm sure your Pa's taking good care of the men from the flatboat," said Mr. Stevenson as he turned back to the wheel. "He's the best doctor I know."

Marie-Grace smiled in agreement as she reached into her pocket. "I have something for Cleopatra," she said, taking out the napkin.

When Cleopatra heard her name, she stood up, stretched, and strolled over to investigate. Her whiskers quivered as Marie-Grace unwrapped the fish. She gobbled the treat and then purred as Marie-Grace patted her.

"I think you've made a friend for life," said Mr. Stevenson, chuckling.

The *Liberty* was moving full speed up the river, and the wind from the open window blew back Marie-Grace's hair. The sun glistened on the water, and tall grasses along the river's edge swayed in the breeze. "The Mississippi is a fine river, isn't it, Mr. Stevenson?" Marie-Grace asked.

"It's the finest river in the world," the pilot agreed. "Sometimes there are dangers, as you saw last night, but there's no place I'd rather be." As the steamboat rounded a curve, Mr. Stevenson rang the bells and said something into the speaking tube.

Another question weighed heavily on Marie-Grace's mind. "Mr. Stevenson," she ventured, "you said that most people aboard steamboats are nice, but sometimes there are cheats and thieves, too. How can you tell who they are?"

"Cheats and thieves can be hard to spot," Mr. Stevenson said, turning the wheel slightly to the left. "But sometimes they give themselves away by lying—or by always being around when things go missing."

Like the book, thought Marie-Grace. "What would the captain do if he found a thief?"

"Well, one time I was on a boat near Baton Rouge when several ladies complained that their jewelry was missing," Mr. Stevenson recalled. "The captain found out who the thief was, and then he threw the fellow right into the river."

Marie-Grace gasped. "Couldn't the thief have drowned?"

"He could have," agreed Mr. Stevenson. "But I heard he made it to the riverbank."

Mr. Stevenson paused as the steamboat approached another bend in the river. "There are some snags ahead," he told Marie-Grace, and he rang the bells to the engine room.

On the way back to her stateroom, Marie-Grace saw Monsieur André sitting along the gallery near the door to her room. He was so busy sketching the riverbank that he seemed lost in his own world. With swift movements, he drew a tree bending along the water, and a hawk circling overhead.

Marie-Grace watched Monsieur André's pencil for a moment. "That's beautiful," she said.

"Thank you," murmured Monsieur André as he finished the outline of the tree. "I have some drawings for sale," he said, motioning to several sketches laid out on the deck beside him. "Beauty is everywhere, but painters must make money."

In one picture, Marie-Grace recognized Mrs. Montjoy strolling with another lady on the deck. Another picture showed Mr. Montjoy, Mr. Hopkins, and Mr. Bold sitting together at a table playing cards. *It looks as if Mr. Bold got Mr. Hopkins to play with them after all,* thought Marie-Grace. *I hope Mr. Hopkins didn't lose too much money.*

"Perhaps your father would like to buy a sketch or a painting," Monsieur André said. "Here is my card." He handed Marie-Grace a cream-colored card that read:

Jacques Paul André

Painter

Canal Street, New Orleans

Trained in Paris

"Thank you," said Marie-Grace, and she pocketed the card. Then she opened the door to her stateroom. After the open air of the pilothouse, the room felt small and stuffy.

Wilhelmina was sitting on the bottom berth. She was squinting as she tried to thread a needle. "Annabelle stopped by while you were gone," said Wilhelmina, glancing up at Marie-Grace. "She said she'd come back later. And I looked for my book again." Wilhelmina put the thread down for a moment and pushed back a strand of hair. "But I still can't find it."

"I noticed something in the book after you went to sleep last night," Marie-Grace said. "Someone had turned down the corners of two of the pages. 'Jack and Jill' was on one page, and 'Little Jack Horner' was on the other. Could 'Jack' be a clue?"

"Maybe," Wilhelmina replied thoughtfully. "My brother's name is John, and some people call him Jack. Everyone at home calls him Johnny, though." She frowned. "But I don't see how Johnny could have anything to do with where Pa hid the gold."

"It wouldn't have to be your brother," said Marie-Grace. "It could be anyone. Oh, wait!" Marie-Grace pulled the painter's card out of her pocket. "Monsieur André's first name is 'Jacques.' That's French for Jack."

Wilhelmina looked at the card. "I don't think it means anything. My Pa never met Monsieur André."

Marie-Grace tried to think of some other possibility. "Do you know anyone named 'Jill'?"

Wilhelmina shook her head. "No, I don't think so." She picked up the needle and tried to thread it. "Ouch!" she said as she pricked her finger. "Drat this needle!"

"Do you want me to thread that?" offered Marie-Grace, glad to do something to help.

"Yes, please," said Wilhelmina. She handed Marie-Grace the needle and a spool of white thread. "I can't see quite as good as I used to. Grammy says it's from sewing so much."

Marie-Grace nodded. "My papa wears eyeglasses to help him see," she said. Standing by the window, she threaded the needle. As she handed it back to Wilhelmina, she asked, "Why *did* you offer to sew Mr. Bold's shirt? I thought you didn't trust him."

"I *don't* trust him," Wilhelmina admitted as she started to sew. "But I want to talk with him. He may have heard my pa say something when he was sick that could be a clue." Wilhelmina sighed. "Besides, Grammy gave me the last of our savings for this trip. I'll sew Mr. Bold's shirt if it means I can earn some money."

Wilhelmina bent over the shirt sleeve. With the material just a few inches from her eyes, she sewed tiny stitches. When she was finished, she handed the shirt to Marie-Grace. "Does this look all right?" she asked.

Marie-Grace sat down next to Wilhelmina and examined the shirt cuff. She could hardly see the rip now. "It looks as good as new," she said admiringly.

Wilhelmina cut and tied the thread and tucked the needle back into the spool of thread. "I'm going to take the shirt back to Mr. Bold now," she said. "Would you come with me?"

Marie-Grace hesitated. She was shy around grown-ups she didn't know. "I'll go as long as I don't have to talk to Mr. Bold," she said.

HITTING A SNAG

"I'll do the talking," promised Wilhelmina. She picked up the shirt. "I have to find out if he knows anything about Pa's gold."

9
A GAMBLE

Marie-Grace felt the deck quiver under her feet as she and Wilhelmina made their way along the gallery. They saw Monsieur André, who was still drawing, as well as lots of other passengers on the deck, but there was no sign of Mr. Bold.

When they reached the open deck at the front of the steamboat, Marie-Grace saw that the *Liberty* was approaching a farm on the riverbank. A sign advertising Wood for Sale stood by tall piles of neatly stacked logs. Marie-Grace knew that steamboats had to stop often and buy wood to fuel their engines. There was always a lot of running and shouting as crew members rushed to bring the wood on board. The men worked as fast as they could so that the steamboat would not be stopped for too long.

"Next stop will be Natchez," a steward announced to the passengers gathered on deck.

Edging their way past the other passengers, the girls circled the steamboat's galleries. They did not find Mr. Bold outside, so they entered the main cabin. At the far end, Mr. Bold was smoking a cigar and playing cards with several other men, including Mr. Montjoy and Mr. Hopkins. Marie-Grace followed Wilhelmina, and the girls stepped from the carpeted floor onto the bare wood of the gentlemen's area.

As they approached the men's table, Marie-Grace heard Mr. Hopkins say, "I'd better stop playing now. I'm getting off the boat at Natchez."

"There's time for one more game, young man," said Mr. Bold, laughing as he collected the money on the table. "Tell you what—why don't we raise the stakes a bit? It will give you a chance to win back all the money you've lost."

"Do you think that's a good idea?" asked Mr. Hopkins, frowning behind his spectacles.

"Of course!" said Mr. Bold. "Let's play one more game. We're just starting to have fun!"

Mr. Montjoy threw down his cards in disgust. *"You're* having fun, Jack, because, for the first time on this trip, you're winning all the money," he complained to Mr. Bold.

None of the men took any notice of the girls until Wilhelmina said, "Excuse me, Mr. Bold, could I speak to you for a moment?"

"Not now, child," said Mr. Bold. He looked irritated. "Can't you see we're busy?"

Marie-Grace felt a blush rise to her cheeks, but Wilhelmina stood her ground. "I want to ask you about my father, Mr. Bold," she said firmly.

The other men at the table stopped their game. Mr. Bold glanced up. "What about him?"

"Do you know if my pa said anything about me when he was sick?"

"No, not that I recall," said Mr. Bold. He smoothed his mustache and looked back down at his cards.

"Are you sure he didn't say anything?" Wilhelmina persisted.

Marie-Grace admired her friend's courage. *I could never speak out like that,* she thought.

But Mr. Bold just nodded without looking up again and added, "Yes, I'm sure."

Wilhelmina gave a frustrated sigh. Then she thrust out the shirt she had been holding. "I finished your mending," she said abruptly. "You owe me ten cents."

"You can put it in my stateroom. I'm in 'Massachusetts,'" said Mr. Bold, waving his hand toward a door on the other side of the main cabin. As he started to shuffle another deck of cards, he added, "I'll give you your money later."

"For goodness' sake, Jack, pay the child the money she's earned now," Mr. Montjoy urged. "You've certainly won enough this morning." Mr. Montjoy reached into Mr. Bold's pile of money and pulled out a quarter. "Here, my dear," he said, handing the coin to Wilhelmina. "I'm sure Mr. Bold will want you to keep the change."

Mr. Bold frowned. For a moment it looked as if he was about to protest. Then he shrugged. "Fine, keep the quarter," he told Wilhelmina. "Just put the shirt in my stateroom." Then he returned to shuffling the deck of cards.

The two girls crossed the gentlemen's area to the stateroom labeled "Massachusetts." The door was unlocked, and when they stepped inside, Marie-Grace saw that it looked just like the stateroom that she and Wilhelmina shared. There was only one small trunk on the floor, though, and the room smelled of cigar smoke.

Wilhelmina folded the shirt and set it on top of the trunk. Both girls had stepped toward the door again when Wilhelmina suddenly stopped. "Marie-Grace, look!" She pointed at the table beside the bed.

On the table was a small cloth-bound book, mostly covered by a handkerchief. Wilhelmina swept aside the handkerchief and eagerly picked up the book.

Could it be the book of nursery rhymes? Marie-Grace wondered.

But Wilhelmina's face fell. "Oh," she said, and she held up the volume for Marie-Grace to see. It was larger than the book of nursery rhymes and had "Ledger" written on the cover.

"My papa has an account book like that in his

office," whispered Marie-Grace. "He keeps track of money in it."

"I thought it was my book," Wilhelmina said with a sigh. She put the ledger back on the table, carefully covering it with the handkerchief.

Marie-Grace heard noises outside the room, and she felt her stomach tighten. *It's not right to be snooping around,* she realized. "We should go," she told Wilhelmina.

"All right," Wilhelmina said reluctantly.

The girls left the stateroom by the gallery door. The *Liberty* was now sailing upriver again. In the distance, Marie-Grace could see buildings near the riverbank. "Look over there," she said to Wilhelmina. "That must be Natchez."

Wilhelmina squinted and then shook her head. "I can't see it yet," she said.

I guess Wilhelmina needs eyeglasses—just as Papa does, thought Marie-Grace. Then she realized what had been different about Mr. Hopkins. "Eyeglasses!" she declared out loud.

"What do you mean?" asked Wilhelmina.

"Mr. Hopkins says he needs to wear

eyeglasses to see. This morning, after the accident, he didn't have his glasses on—but he was the only one besides me who saw Annabelle down on the deck. Don't you think that's odd?"

"Yes, that is odd," Wilhelmina agreed. "I remember him saying that he *always* wears eyeglasses."

Did Mr. Hopkins tell the truth about needing eyeglasses? Marie-Grace wondered.

Wilhelmina stared out at the river for a moment. Suddenly, she turned to Marie-Grace, her eyes flashing. "Was Mr. Hopkins wearing eyeglasses just now, when we saw him playing cards?" she asked.

"I think so," said Marie-Grace. "I'm not sure."

"Let's go find out," Wilhelmina urged. "He could be trying to trick us," she said as she headed back toward the main cabin.

"Wait," cried Marie-Grace, hurrying to catch up with her friend. "We don't know that Mr. Hopkins has done anything wrong," she whispered to Wilhelmina.

"Maybe not," Wilhelmina whispered back.

"But if he's not wearing his glasses now, and he can see the cards anyway, then we'll know he hasn't been telling the truth about himself."

When the girls entered the main cabin, they saw that most of the card players were gone. The waiters were setting the tables and getting the room ready for the midday meal. Only Mr. Montjoy and Mr. Bold were still there, smoking cigars and looking glum.

Wilhelmina headed straight for the men. "Excuse me, but do you know where Mr. Hopkins is?" she asked.

"No, and I don't care!" exploded Mr. Bold. "That young fellow pretended that he didn't know how to play cards. But he tricked me and took all my money!"

Mr. Montjoy shook his bald head. "Now, don't be a bad loser, Jack," he told Mr. Bold. "The boy just called your bluff on the last game, that's all." Mr. Montjoy turned to Marie-Grace and Wilhelmina. "Mr. Hopkins is getting off the boat at Natchez. I expect he's on deck."

Marie-Grace's mind was whirling as she

and Wilhelmina headed back out to the open promenade. *Mr. Hopkins said he wasn't good at playing cards,* she thought. *But he beat Mr. Bold, who plays cards a lot. Has Mr. Hopkins told the truth about* anything?

Wilhelmina seemed to read her mind. "I don't think Mr. Hopkins can be trusted," she said, walking quickly. "Maybe he's the thief."

Marie-Grace's stomach twisted. "But he helped me with Annabelle," she reminded Wilhelmina.

"Yes, but he still could have taken my book," Wilhelmina whispered.

Passengers were gathering by the railing to take their first look at the town, and Marie-Grace saw the roofs of Natchez growing closer. Wilhelmina spotted Mr. Hopkins standing at the back of the deck with a brown leather bag by his side. "Mr. Hopkins!" she called, hurrying over to him.

Marie-Grace followed close behind. She saw that Mr. Hopkins was not wearing his eyeglasses.

Mr. Hopkins tipped his hat politely to the

girls. "I hope you young ladies have a pleasant journey up the river," he said, smiling. "I'm departing the steamboat here at Natchez."

"Yes, we know," said Wilhelmina impatiently. "We need to ask you something. Marie-Grace says that you weren't wearing your eyeglasses this morning when the boat stopped for the accident. But you saw Annabelle down on the main deck anyway. And you're not wearing your eyeglasses now. Does that mean you don't really need eyeglasses?"

Mr. Hopkins looked surprised by the question. "Why yes, I *do* need my eyeglasses to read and see things close up," he replied. "But I can see faraway things just fine." He pointed into the distance. "Look, there's a red barn over there—just beyond those trees."

Marie-Grace looked and then nodded. "He's right," she told Wilhelmina. She remembered her father telling her that some people need glasses to see things far away, but others need them only to see close up. Her face grew hot with embarrassment. *We were wrong about Mr. Hopkins*, Marie-Grace realized. *He was telling the truth.*

The steamboat's whistle blew shrilly, and people began moving toward the gangplank. "Looks like we're arriving," said Mr. Hopkins.

Wilhelmina, however, did not give up so easily. "Mr. Bold said that you were only pretending that you didn't know how to play cards," she said. "He says you tricked him and took all his money!"

Mr. Hopkins grinned at the girls. "Maybe I do know how to play cards a little better than I let on," he admitted. He lowered his voice. "But the only people who lose money to me are the ones who try to take advantage of a newcomer."

"Like Mr. Bold?" guessed Marie-Grace.

"That's right," said Mr. Hopkins. "He's a greedy man, and he tried to cheat me. Unfortunately for him, it wasn't as easy as he thought it would be."

"What about my book of nursery rhymes?" demanded Wilhelmina boldly. "Did you take it?"

"I don't know anything about a book,"

Mr. Hopkins said. He looked confused. "What would I do with nursery rhymes?"

Wilhelmina looked doubtful. "So it wasn't you?"

"Of course not," Mr. Hopkins assured her. "I've never taken anything from a child in my life."

Before Wilhelmina could ask another question, Mr. Hopkins reached down for the bag at his side. "Now, if you girls will excuse me, I'm off to see Natchez." He tipped his hat to them again. "Farewell!"

While birds swooped overhead, Marie-Grace watched Mr. Hopkins walk off the gangplank. She had a sinking feeling. *If Mr. Hopkins didn't take the book, who did?*

10

LOST AND FOUND

There was a flurry of activity on the *Liberty*.
As soon as the departing passengers and cargo
were gone, new passengers and cargo came
aboard. Marie-Grace and Wilhelmina watched
as porters carried trunks and boxes and crew
members loaded livestock. Two men carried
several small pigs onto the boat, followed by
a dozen crates of chickens. The hens cackled
loudly, and a rooster crowed out, *cockadoodledoo.*

Marie-Grace heard someone call her name.
She turned to see Annabelle with her mother and
baby sister. Annabelle let go of her mother's hand
and rushed toward the girls, her blonde curls
blowing in the wind.

"Look what I have," Annabelle cried, holding
something in the air.

Marie-Grace gasped. It was the book of nursery rhymes!

"How did you get this?" Wilhelmina demanded, snatching the book from Annabelle.

"I found it," Annabelle said proudly.

"You didn't find it in our stateroom last night, did you, Annabelle?" Marie-Grace asked gently.

"No, it was on the deck, outside your door." Annabelle pointed down the length of the gallery. "It was on the ground, by the chair. I saw it when I went to your room today and you weren't there."

"Why didn't you bring it to me right away?" Wilhelmina asked her.

Annabelle's eyes widened. "I didn't know it was yours! I took it to Mama, because I wanted her to read it to me. But she said your name is on it, so I should give it to you."

Mrs. Rumsford called for Annabelle, but the little girl turned to Marie-Grace. "Will you read me the book?"

"Yes, later," Marie-Grace answered absentmindedly before Annabelle ran to join her mother. "How did the book end up on the floor outside our room?" Marie-Grace whispered to her friend as they hurried back to their stateroom.

"I don't know," said Wilhelmina. "I'm *sure* that I left it in the room."

Marie-Grace remembered that Monsieur André had been sketching outside their room. She wondered if the painter might have taken the book. *Could he be looking for the gold?* she wondered. *He did say that he needed money.* But she dismissed this idea. She had suspected Mr. Hopkins of being a thief and had been wrong. She didn't want to make the same mistake with Monsieur André.

As soon as the girls reached their stateroom, they sat down and studied the book together. Marie-Grace showed Wilhelmina the pages with the corners that had been turned down. There was a drawing of Jack and Jill going up the hill together. *Could that mean something?* she wondered. *Or what about the picture of Little Miss Muffet? Or the cat playing a fiddle?*

"The cat has a fiddle, and your pa had a violin," Marie-Grace said. "Could that be a clue?"

"I think a fiddle is the same thing as a violin," said Wilhelmina, looking at the picture. "But I already looked at Pa's violin—and the case, too. There's no gold there. They're not heavy enough."

"There might be a clue hidden in them," Marie-Grace insisted. "Maybe inside the violin."

"It's possible," Wilhelmina said with growing excitement. "Let's look!"

Wilhelmina pulled the violin out of her trunk, and both girls examined the instrument carefully. Then they searched the old violin case. Marie-Grace had hoped they might find a hidden scrap of paper or a message scratched into the case, but there was nothing.

"Was there a special song your pa used to play?" Marie-Grace asked hopefully. "Could that be a clue?"

Wilhelmina shook her head. "He played lots of songs. I don't remember any special favorites."

There was a knock at the door. Wilhelmina quickly put the violin away and closed her trunk before answering. "Who is it?" she called.

"Me!" Annabelle announced. Marie-Grace opened the door and the little girl burst into the room. "Mama's busy with the baby, but she told me I could come and play with you," Annabelle said breathlessly.

"I'm sorry, but we're busy, too," Marie-Grace told her. "I'll play later—I promise."

"You said that before!" protested Annabelle. She picked up the book of nursery rhymes from the bed. "You said you'd read this to me."

Marie-Grace glanced at Wilhelmina. "Do you mind if we borrow the book? I'll read it to Annabelle outside."

Wilhelmina nodded. "I'll keep looking here."

Marie-Grace followed Annabelle out to the gallery, and they settled on wooden chairs, and Marie-Grace began reading. "There was an old woman who lived in a shoe . . ."

"Isn't that a silly place to live?" interrupted Annabelle.

"Yes," Marie-Grace agreed. "Especially if you have a big family."

As the river flowed by peacefully, Annabelle asked questions about every rhyme Marie-Grace read to her. And when they reached the page with the turned-down corner, Annabelle asked, "Why did someone draw there?"

"Where?"

"There." Annabelle pointed an accusing finger to the bottom of the left-hand page.

Marie-Grace looked closely. She saw that Annabelle was pointing to a tiny mark that had been drawn very lightly in pencil. A similar mark was at the bottom of the facing page. Marie-Grace quickly leafed through the other pages, but none of them were marked.

"My mama says that I shouldn't write in books," Annabelle said solemnly. "Why did someone write in this book?"

"I'm not sure," said Marie-Grace as the river breeze fluttered the pages. "Let's go show this to Wilhelmina."

11
MAGIC NIGHT

That evening, clouds rolled in and rain came pouring down. In her stateroom, Marie-Grace worked on her letter to Cécile. She explained all about the missing gold, writing that she and Wilhelmina had spent the entire afternoon looking for clues in the book but hadn't had any success. When she heard the supper bell, Marie-Grace carefully blotted the ink and put the letter away in her trunk.

Wilhelmina, who had been lying on her bed, sat up. "I feel like a failure," she announced, snapping the book of nursery rhymes closed. "I was sure that the book held the clues as to where Pa hid the gold, but I didn't even see these marks before. Now I see them, but I still don't know what they mean!"

"It's not your fault," Marie-Grace told her. "The marks are hard to see. I'm sure your pa didn't want other people to notice them."

"But he counted on *me* to notice—and I didn't," protested Wilhelmina. She shook her head sadly. "I still don't know what riddle Pa was talking about. Maybe"—she paused—"maybe Pa was too sick to leave me clues. Maybe I'll never find the gold."

Marie-Grace listened to the rain spattering on the deck. She wished with all her heart that she could help her friend. "What will your family do?" Marie-Grace asked anxiously.

Wilhelmina stood up. "I've thought about it, and I've decided to sell Pa's pots and pans and things when I get back to New Madrid. We don't need them, and they'll buy us food for a while."

Marie-Grace shivered as if a cold wind had swept over her. *Without the gold, how long will Wilhelmina's family be able to stay together?* she wondered.

The girls entered the main cabin for supper, and Marie-Grace was glad to see her father, Sister Frederica, and Sister Catherine seated at the table. "How are the injured men, Papa?"

"They're improving," Papa replied. "Caleb had been running a fever, but he's resting more comfortably now."

"Oh, good," said Mrs. Montjoy. "Well, I hope you'll all be able to join us for our special entertainment this evening." She looked around the table, beaming proudly. "Reggie will be doing his famous magic tricks!"

The magic show! thought Marie-Grace. *I'd completely forgotten.*

"Monsieur André has also agreed to display some of his drawings," Mrs. Montjoy continued. "And after all the work you've done for those poor wounded men, Dr. Gardner, you must take a seat in the front row."

"Thank you, ma'am," said Papa politely. "I'll check on our patients after supper. If they are still resting, I'd like very much to attend." He smiled at Marie-Grace and Wilhelmina. "I'm sure you girls would enjoy a magic show, wouldn't you?"

Marie-Grace thought it sounded exciting. "Yes, Papa!" she said. "I'd like that."

But Wilhelmina shook her head. "No, thank you," she said.

Mr. Bold looked up in surprise. "What's wrong?" he asked as he chewed his food. "You're not sick, are you?"

"No," Wilhelmina replied. She bent over her food again. "I have other things to do."

Papa and the nuns excused themselves as coffee was being served, and Wilhelmina stood up, too. "I'm going back to the room," she whispered to Marie-Grace.

After supper was cleared away, the waiters began to rearrange the furniture. They set a large table covered with a velvet cloth at the forward end of the cabin and lined up several rows of chairs facing the table. Monsieur André arranged his drawings along both sides of the room, and he put out a sign announcing that the sketches were available for purchase.

Marie-Grace joined the passengers who gathered to admire the drawings. The sketches depicted scenes of the river and life aboard the *Liberty*—crew members hauling ropes, men playing cards, and couples ambling on deck.

"They're so lifelike!" murmured one lady.

"Why, this one captures the very spirit of the river!" exclaimed another lady. "I wonder how much it costs."

As Marie-Grace strolled by the pictures, Annabelle ran up to join her. "Look, Marie-Grace," she said, pointing at a drawing. "Mama's in that picture, and I am, too!"

"I see you!" said Marie-Grace, studying the sketch. It showed several passengers sitting along the gallery in the open air. Mrs. Rumsford was holding her baby, and Annabelle, holding Priscilla, was perched on a chair beside her mother. Annabelle's round face and bouncy curls reminded Marie-Grace of the illustration in the nursery rhyme book. "You look like Little Miss Muffet," Marie-Grace told Annabelle, smiling.

"But I'm sitting on a chair, not a tuffet,"

Annabelle corrected her solemnly. "And there's no spider either." She hugged her doll close to her. "Priscilla and I don't like spiders."

"You're right," agreed Marie-Grace. "There's no spider."

Marie-Grace was glad to see her father arrive in time for the show. He waved cheerfully to Marie-Grace, who had taken a seat with Annabelle and her mother. Mrs. Montjoy, who was seated at the piano, motioned Papa to an empty seat in the front row.

A moment later, Mrs. Montjoy played a thundering chord on the piano as Mr. Montjoy approached the table. The short, bald man had been transformed by a tall black hat and long black cape. *He looks as if he really could do magic*, Marie-Grace thought with surprise.

"Ladies and gentlemen!" Mr. Montjoy called out in a deep voice. The chatter in the room faded. "We are pleased to bring to you a night of magic!"

Everyone applauded. Mr. Montjoy bowed gallantly. He tipped his hat and showed the audience it was empty. "Nothing is as it appears to be," intoned Mr. Montjoy. He put his hat on the table and swished his cape over it. Then he reached inside the hat and pulled out a white rabbit.

"Ahhh!" gasped Annabelle.

The audience applauded while the rabbit, its whiskers twitching, began to explore the velvet-covered table.

"Dear, dear!" exclaimed Mr. Montjoy, pretending to be surprised. "We can't have a rabbit hopping about. Back you go." He gently put the rabbit into his hat and, after another swish of his cape, showed the hat to the audience. Once again, it was empty. Everyone clapped enthusiastically.

"Thank you," said Mr. Montjoy, bowing deeply. "And now I shall make solid gold"—he paused dramatically—"disappear!"

Marie-Grace leaned forward. *I wish I knew how to make Wilhelmina's gold reappear*, she thought.

Mr. Montjoy pulled a gold coin from his pocket and showed both sides of it to the audience. Then he passed the gold coin around to Papa and several other people in the front row. "Just an ordinary coin, isn't it?" he asked them. The audience members agreed.

With a flourish, Mr. Montjoy held the coin up in the air in his right hand. Then he closed his left hand around the coin and said a few words that Marie-Grace did not understand. When he opened both hands, the coin had vanished.

"Ooooooh!" exclaimed Annabelle.

Mr. Montjoy showed the audience his empty hands and the empty table. Then he pointed to a distinguished-looking man in the front row. "Do you have my gold coin, sir?"

The man looked surprised. "No, sir, I do not."

"Will you swear to that?"

The man frowned. "Of course."

"Ah, but you're mistaken," said Mr. Montjoy, striding over to the man. With one swift movement, the magician pulled the coin from behind the man's ear. Then he waved the coin in front of the audience.

"Why, that's . . . that's impossible!" the man

121

sputtered. "How did you do that?"

"Nothing is as it appears to be!" Mr. Montjoy reminded him, smiling mysteriously.

The audience applauded, and Annabelle, her eyes wide with surprise, clapped so hard that her blonde curls bobbed up and down. *She really does look like Miss Muffet,* thought Marie-Grace again. She recited the rhyme to herself. "Little Miss Muffet, she sat on a tuffet, eating . . ." Then her hand flew to her mouth. "Goodness gracious!" she exclaimed.

"What?" asked Annabelle, turning to face Marie-Grace.

"I have to go," Marie-Grace whispered. "You stay here with your mother." At the front of the room, Mr. Montjoy was beginning his next trick. Marie-Grace quietly ducked out of the room, and then she half walked, half ran to her stateroom. *I have to tell Wilhelmina!* she thought. *I think I know what the clue is!*

12
DESPERATE SEARCH

"Wilhelmina!" Marie-Grace declared, bursting into the stateroom. "Maybe it's the spider!"

"Spider?" repeated Wilhelmina. She was lying on her bed, reading the nursery rhymes. Now she looked around as if she expected to see a web hanging over her head. "Where?"

"There's a spider in the rhyme," said Marie-Grace, closing the door behind her. "Your father has that cooking pot called a spider. Maybe that's the clue we've been looking for!"

"There might be something written on the spider in Pa's trunk," Wilhelmina said. She put the book aside and sat up eagerly. "Let's go look!"

Suddenly, Marie-Grace heard a noise. The sound had come from the gallery outside the girls' stateroom. She put her finger to her lips, warning Wilhelmina to be quiet. Then she tiptoed over to the window and peeked through the curtains. Through the rain, she could see that the *Liberty* was heading toward the riverbank. Marie-Grace listened for a moment, but all she could hear was the pounding rain and gusting wind.

Marie-Grace dropped the curtain. "I guess it was just the wind," she said. She crossed the room and sat on the bed next to her friend. "It looks as if we're stopping for wood. Let's wait until morning to go down to the main deck. My papa will go with us then."

"No, let's go *now*," Wilhelmina insisted. "We have to find out if the spider is the clue."

Marie-Grace shook her head. "Papa's at the magic show," she said. "And it's raining."

"The weather doesn't matter," said Wilhelmina, standing up. "And since we're stopping for wood, the crew will be busy. They won't notice that we're on the main deck."

I should get Papa, Marie-Grace thought. *But what if I'm wrong about the spider, just as I was wrong about the fiddle?*

Wilhelmina saw her hesitation. "If you're right, we could finally find the gold!"

"But if a crew member sees us, we could get into a lot of trouble," Marie-Grace argued.

"I have an idea," Wilhelmina said suddenly. She grabbed her shawl and draped it over her head. It looked like the scarves that many of the women on the main deck wore to cover their heads. "If we wear our shawls like this, no one will know who we are!"

Marie-Grace felt the steamboat lurch to a stop. She knew that the crew would soon be rushing off the boat to get the wood from the shore. Marie-Grace pulled her own shawl over her head and nodded. "All right," she said. "Let's hurry."

Without another word, the two girls slipped out onto the deserted gallery. The rain was falling harder now. As she followed Wilhelmina down the stairs, Marie-Grace heard applause and laughter coming from the main cabin.

At the bottom deck, Marie-Grace heard a man

shout, "Bring the wood as fast as you can, men!" Lanterns were burning along the gangplank, and by the dim light, Marie-Grace saw crew members rushing back and forth in the rain.

Most of the deck passengers were under shelter from the downpour. Some had put up makeshift tents, and others were huddled around a cookstove with soggy blankets pulled over their heads. No one paid attention to the two girls as they picked their way across the crowded deck.

The girls finally reached the passage where Wilhelmina's trunk was stored. The engines were quiet now, and the paddle wheels had stopped. Light seeped from the door of the nearby engine room, and Marie-Grace was surprised to see that crates were piled even higher than they had been the night before. *They've put more cargo down here,* she realized as she followed Wilhelmina down the narrow passage. The walkway smelled of hay mixed with manure.

Suddenly, Wilhelmina stopped short. "Hide!" she whispered.

Marie-Grace quickly ducked behind a barrel.

Wilhelmina scrambled in beside her. Marie-Grace felt her heart pounding as she crouched down in the darkness. "What's wrong?" she whispered to Wilhelmina.

"Someone's there!"

Marie-Grace peeked out from behind the barrel. There, in the middle of the walkway, was the shadowy figure of a man. He was trying to pick the lock on Wilhelmina's trunk. He was so intent on his task that he hadn't noticed the girls.

"Let's go back upstairs," Marie-Grace whispered. "We'll get help."

"He could be stealing Pa's gold!" Wilhelmina whispered ugently. She stood up. "I've got to stop him."

Marie-Grace knew it wouldn't be brave for them to face this thief on their own—it would be foolish. "No! It's too dangerous," she insisted.

Wilhelmina whirled around to face Marie-Grace, and her shawl caught on one of the crates. The crate rattled as Wilhelmina tried to tug the fabric loose. Finally, she ripped the shawl free, disturbing the chickens inside the crate.

The birds began to cluck and squawk. Then the rooster gave a piercing crow. Both girls froze.

"Who's there?" said the man.

Marie-Grace recognized the voice. *It's Mr. Bold!* She felt her heart pounding. She wanted to yell for help, but it was so noisy on deck that she was afaid no one would hear her.

"Who's there?" Mr. Bold demanded again, walking toward the clucking chickens.

We have to get away from here! Marie-Grace realized. She tugged Wilhelmina's arm. "Come on!"

In a blur of panic, Marie-Grace led the way back down the narrow walkway, past the barrels and boxes crammed into the narrow space. As the girls ran out onto the open deck, Marie-Grace cried, "Help!" But amid the noise and confusion of the men loading wood in the pouring rain, no one paid attention.

Marie-Grace saw the door to the engine room half open. "In here!" she directed Wilhelmina.

The room was empty except for an old man standing by the engines. "There's a thief out there!" Wilhelmina shouted to the man. "You've got to stop him!"

The old man looked confused. "I don't understand," he said in a thick accent. "What is wrong?"

While Wilhelmina tried to explain, Marie-Grace heard a bell. Then a familiar voice came through the speaking tube. It was Mr. Stevenson from the pilothouse.

Marie-Grace ran to the speaking tube. "Mr. Stevenson—it's Marie-Grace. Please help us!"

13
THE KEY

A few moments later, Mr. Stevenson and Papa ran into the engine room. "You're not hurt, are you?" Papa asked breathlessly. "What happened?"

"We're all right," Marie-Grace assured him.

"It's Mr. Bold!" Wilhelmina declared. She pointed out the door. "He's trying to steal my father's gold. You have to stop him!"

"We saw him trying to open the trunk," Marie-Grace added.

Papa and Mr. Stevenson exchanged a glance. "Wait here, girls," Papa said.

Marie-Grace heard shouting outside and a loud crash. *I hope no one gets hurt*, she thought. Wilhelmina looked as scared as Marie-Grace felt. "Don't worry," Marie-Grace said, trying to comfort her friend. "It will be all right."

Wilhelmina noodead, her face pale in the flickering light of the oil lamps.

Marie-Grace listened for more noises, but she heard only the sounds of the crew bringing on wood. When her father and Mr. Stevenson finally returned, their clothes were wet from the rain.

"We found Mr. Bold," Mr. Stevenson reported. "He was trying to hide, but when we caught him, he admitted that he'd been looking for the gold."

"And you were right about the book, Grace," Papa said. "Mr. Bold took it. He said he didn't find any clues, so he left the book outside your room. He was hoping that you and Wilhelmina would find the gold and lead him to it."

The girls looked at each other. "If Mr. Bold didn't know where the gold was, why was he looking in the trunk?" Marie-Grace asked.

"He claimed that he'd lost a lot of money playing cards," Mr. Stevenson explained. "Since everyone was at the magic show, he took the chance to look through Mr. Newman's trunk."

"That weasel!" Wilhelmina said angrily. She

looked out the open door. "Where is he?"

"A crew member is taking him to see the captain," said Mr. Stevenson.

Just then, however, Captain Smith appeared in the doorway. His gray eyebrows were knit together in a deep frown. "Mr. Bold just jumped in the river and swam ashore—and then he ran away." Captain Smith shook his head. "What in tarnation is going on?"

Before anyone could answer, several crew members filed into the engine room. They looked curiously at the group gathered in the crowded room. "It looks as though the wood is on board now, sir," Mr. Stevenson said. "I think we'd better go up to the main cabin. We can explain everything up there."

"But we'll need my father's trunk—the big one!" said Wilhelmina.

"It's very important," Marie-Grace pleaded. "We think we finally have the clue to the gold."

Captain Smith frowned, but he pointed at two of the crew members. "Bring the trunk up to the main cabin," he ordered. "And be quick about it."

Marie-Grace and Wilhelmina stood side by side in the main cabin and watched anxiously as Mr. Newman's trunk was carried in. There had been so much cargo in the passageway that it had taken the men more than an hour to get the trunk out.

The magic show had ended long ago. All that remained of the evening's entertainment was the velvet-covered table at the front of the cabin. Captain Smith directed the crew members to place the trunk in front of the table and to bring a pair of lanterns.

Wilhelmina pulled the key from her pocket and opened the trunk's lid. Marie-Grace helped her friend drag the thick blankets out of the trunk. *I hope I wasn't wrong about the spider,* she worried as she watched Wilhelmina reach for the black pot. *What if it's not the clue after all?*

"It sure is heavy," said Wilhelmina, pulling out the spider.

Marie-Grace felt her heart racing as she

peered at the pot. She didn't see any writing on it. "Let's look on the bottom," she suggested.

Wilhelmina turned the pot over, and she and Marie-Grace studied it. Papa and Captain Smith leaned in for a closer look, too. "I don't see anything special about it," said the captain gruffly.

Marie-Grace ran her fingers over the spider. It felt as if something was flaking off the bottom of the pot. "Is there paint on this?" she asked.

Wilhelmina touched the pot, too. "It does feel that way," she agreed. "Why would Pa have painted a cooking pot?"

Marie-Grace remembered Mr. Montjoy's words: *"Nothing is as it appears to be,"* the magician had warned. "Maybe there's something under the paint," she suggested.

"Well, that's easy enough to find out," said Mr. Stevenson. He took the spider from Wilhelmina and put it on the table. Then he took a small folding knife out of his pocket and carefully cut into the surface. Marie-Grace held the lantern up to the pot. There, below the paint, was a sliver of warm yellow shine.

"Gracious sakes!" Marie-Grace whispered.

"Well, I'll be hornswoggled!" declared Captain Smith.

With trembling fingers, Wilhelmina peeled off the paint. The spider was made of solid gold, covered with a thin layer of black paint—just enough to make it look like an ordinary iron pot.

"Oh, Marie-Grace, we found it!" Wilhelmina cried joyfully. "We finally found the gold!"

Quickly, the girls searched the trunk again. The other pots were made of iron, but the frying pan, covered with the same flaking paint, was also solid gold.

"That's the pan that Pa used for flapjacks!" Wilhelmina exclaimed. "Jack *was* a clue!"

The heavy serving spoon turned out to be gold, too. "And the dish ran after the spoon," Marie-Grace recited. She smiled happily. "Of course."

But when she looked at Wilhelmina, her smile disappeared. Her friend, who had been brave for so long, now had tears rolling down her face. "What's wrong?" Marie-Grace asked gently. "We found the gold. Isn't it what you wanted?"

"Yes," said Wilhelmina. "But—" she choked back a sob. "Pa will never *know* that we found it. He'll never know our family can stay together now, either."

"Your father had trust in you, Wilhelmina," Marie Grace's father told her. "I'm sure he knew your family would be all right."

"He knew you'd be able to solve one more riddle, too," Marie-Grace added. "And you did!"

"You and I solved it together," Wilhelmina said. She reached out and clasped Marie-Grace's hand. "Thank you."

On Friday afternoon, Marie-Grace and Wilhelmina stood together at the deck railing as the *Liberty* rounded a bend in the Mississippi River. New Madrid was just ahead. The passengers cheered as the whistle blew and the town's buildings came into sight.

The wounded men from the flatboat were the first to leave the boat. Their families were waiting to meet them on the levee, and Papa went ashore to explain everything that had happened. Two of the men could walk ashore with help, while Caleb was carried on a stretcher.

Annabelle's father was waiting on shore to meet his family. Annabelle waved to him, and then she hugged Marie-Grace. "I'll miss you!" the little girl whispered.

"I'll miss you, too, Annabelle," said Marie-Grace, smiling. "Take good care of Priscilla!"

"I will," promised Annabelle, and she held tight to her doll as she followed her mother and baby sister down the steps and across the gangplank.

Then it was Wilhelmina's turn to go. She was wearing the same brown calico dress and shawl that she'd worn when she boarded the boat in New Orleans, but she no longer looked tired and hungry. Her cheeks were now pink, and her eyes were bright.

Marie-Grace handed her an envelope that held the letter she had written to Cécile. "Are you sure you don't mind sending this for me?"

"I don't mind at all. I'll take it to the post this very day," said Wilhelmina. "After all you've done to help me, I'm happy to help you. And remember to visit us when you come back down the river."

"I will," Marie-Grace said happily. "Papa said we can stop on our way home."

After the two girls hugged, Wilhelmina followed the two porters who carried her trunks ashore. From the boiler deck, Marie-Grace watched Wilhelmina's two red-haired brothers race across the levee to hug their big sister.

Now their family can stay together, thought Marie-Grace as she brushed tears of happiness from her eyes. *Her pa would have been very glad.*

The *Liberty*'s whistle blew, and Papa came back on board. He and Marie-Grace stayed at the deck railing until the steamboat left New Madrid. Then they went up to the pilothouse to see Mr. Stevenson.

Cleopatra strolled over to Marie-Grace as soon as she entered the pilothouse. While Marie-Grace scratched the cat's chin, she thanked Mr. Stevenson again for all his help. "If you and Papa hadn't come down when you did, Mr. Bold might've gotten away with Wilhelmina's gold."

"Well, it's a good thing you girls found where it was hidden," said Mr. Stevenson.

"Yes," said Marie-Grace. She shivered at the thought that Wilhelmina might have sold the pots and pans without ever realizing their value. "I wonder how her father was able to make those things out of gold."

"Oh, if Mr. Newman had worked as a blacksmith, it would have been easy enough," said Papa, pouring himself a cup of coffee from the stove. "He probably chose the spider and the frying pan because iron is naturally heavy. Nobody would've suspected that they were really gold, especially since he kept them with his other pots and pans. The gold might not have been discovered for a long time if you and Wilhelmina hadn't searched so hard."

Mr. Stevenson rang the bells to the engine room. "We're making good time," he said with a smile. "We should be in Cairo, Illinois, by tomorrow."

As Marie-Grace looked out the window, she saw the river stretched in front of her, with the sun shining on the water. She'd never been so far north on the Mississippi before, and she wondered what Cairo would be like.

I'll tell Cécile all about it in my next letter, she thought happily. Then she leaned forward to see what might be around the next turn in the river.

Looking Back

A Peek into the Past

The busy port of New Orleans in 1854

When Marie-Grace was growing up, the Mississippi River was known as America's highway. More than 2,000 miles long, the river was the main route across the country, winding its way from Minnesota in the north past New Orleans to the southern tip of Louisiana. During the 1850s, the Mississippi was crowded with flatboats, rafts, and keelboats, all of which were dwarfed by the larger and more powerful steamboats.

Marie-Grace had never been on a boat as large or as elegant as the *Liberty*. Many steamboats were as fancy as the best homes and hotels

Workers loading cargo onto the main *deck. The second level is called the* boiler *deck, and the* hurricane *deck is above the boiler deck.*

in America. In fact, steamboats were sometimes called "floating palaces" or "moving hotels." Staterooms were small, but they were decorated with fine furnishings. The steamboat's main cabin was even more splendid. The long room dazzled passengers with graceful architecture, colored-glass skylights, and sparkling chandeliers. Upholstered sofas and chairs were arranged around tables for reading, letter writing, or conversation. At mealtime, the furniture was rearranged to form a dining hall.

A luxurious main cabin

The main cabin was the social center of the boat. There, passengers might be entertained with lectures, concerts, and even balls. The ladies' cabin was at one end and

The popularity of steamboat travel was reflected in decorative items, such as this vase, during the 1800s.

usually featured a piano for entertainment. The gentlemen's cabin at the other end included a bar and sometimes even a barbershop.

Card games were the primary pastime in the gentlemen's cabin. Travelers ran the risk of unknowingly playing with professional gamblers. These gamblers boarded a steamboat at one port, won money from unsuspecting passengers, and then quietly slipped off the boat at another port—just as Mr. Hopkins did.

Travel by steamboat was luxurious and lively,

Many boats posted signs warning men who played cards for money to do so at their own risk.

but it could also be quite dangerous. To power the boats, crew members constantly fed wood into the furnaces. The furnaces heated boilers, creating steam. If the pressure in the boilers built up, they could explode. Steamboats were

made of wood, so they were easily destroyed by fire. Highly flammable cargo, such as cotton, made boiler accidents even worse.

Fire wasn't the only danger. When the river was covered with a foggy mist, smaller flatboats and rafts were nearly invisible to steamboat pilots. A collision might damage the steamboat, but it could completely wreck a smaller vessel and seriously injure its passengers, as happened on Marie-Grace's trip.

Steamboats could also collide with one

This raftsman is trying desperately to signal to the approaching steamboat.

The view from the pilothouse. The speaking tube, which crew members used to communicate with the engine room, is to the right of the pilot.

another. Pilots communicated where they were and where they were going through a series of whistles. One whistle meant a boat was passing on the *starboard*, or right side. Two whistles signaled a *larboard,* or left-side, pass. When river traffic was heavy, mistaken signals could cause accidents rather than prevent them.

Navigating boats up and down the Mississippi wasn't easy. The river was full of

Samuel Clemens, better known as author Mark Twain, was a steamboat pilot in the 1860s. His novel The Adventures of Huckleberry Finn *is set on the Mississippi River.*

winding curves and narrow passages. Shallow waters could trap a boat, and hidden tree stumps and other *snags*, or obstacles, could cause serious damage and even sink a vessel. Strong winds and currents could take a boat off course. Steering a steamboat required careful observation and good judgment. Steamboat pilots, like Mr. Stevenson and Marie-Grace's Uncle Luc, were highly respected for their knowledge of the river.

By the early 1900s, safer and more efficient forms of transportation put an end to the steamboat era. But this unique part of America's past is not forgotten. You can still enjoy a cruise on an authentic steamboat in several cities along the Mississippi River—including New Orleans.

How to Pronounce French Names

Cécile *(say-seel)*

Grand Théâtre *(grahn tay-ah-truh)*

Jacques Paul André *(zhahk pohl ahn-dray)*

Luc *(lewk)*

Monsieur *(muh-syuh)*

Océane *(oh-say-ahn)*

About the Author

 Sarah Masters Buckey grew up in New Jersey, where her favorite hobbies were swimming in the summer, sledding in the winter, and reading all year round. She liked to read so much that whenever her parents packed their car for a vacation, her mother would include a grocery bag filled with library books just for her. As a writer, she's enjoyed living in different parts of the United States, including fifteen years in Texas.

Ms. Buckey loves writing for children, and five of her novels have been nominated for awards. She and her family now make their home in New Hampshire.